T0193608

John "Jack" Brown
Voiced by the Women Who Knew Him

Daniel MacPherson

WESTBOW
PRESS®
A DIVISION OF THOMAS NELSON
& ZONDERVAN

WestBow Press books may be ordered through booksellers or by contacting:

WestBow Press
A Division of Thomas Nelson & Zondervan
1663 Liberty Drive
Bloomington, IN 47403
www.westbowpress.com
1 (866) 928-1240

ISBN: 978-1-9736-1626-9 (sc)
ISBN: 978-1-9736-1625-2 (e)

Library of Congress Control Number: 2018900189

Print information available on the last page.

WestBow Press rev. date: 1/11/2018

Introduction

Fifteen years ago, the editor of the newspaper where I worked asked me to write an obituary for John "Jack" Brown. I had heard his name in social circles, but he was not politically active, so I knew nothing about him before working on this story. Jack resided in a small township outside the county seat of Medina, Ohio, and he amassed a small fortune while on the earth. Some of it was in material wealth, most of it in the love from the people he touched. Whether a girlfriend or a business partner, folks found it was easy to trust Jack.

Jack Brown was married for twenty-four years and had one daughter, a secretary, and four mistresses after the death of his wife. Of the seven women close to him, only one ever really knew him. She could look past his bravado to see the scared little boy who hides in every man. His charm was not wasted on her, but it could not deceive her. The embrace she had on him prevented any of his girlfriends from having him entirely in the ten years after her death. His dependence on her was so deep, it may have led to her demise. Although the girlfriends could be with him, hold him, and even love him, they could never truly have him.

After his funeral, I met several of his girlfriends and his daughter at a diner next to the funeral home. His daughter, Katherine, knew he had female friends but was surprised by how many and the feelings they had for her dad. Their reverence, admiration, and conviction impressed me. Jack had a strong, commanding presence. My biggest disappointment was not meeting him.

I wrote a feature on Jack, which my editor reduced to about a tenth of its original size. I found it very hard to keep the article brief, after listening to these women. My original story would have covered about three-quarters of a page. I knew this was more than any newspaper would permit, but I believed Jack's story was something special.

A couple days after my editor dismantled my article, I decided to write this book about Jack Brown. Everyone at the diner that evening agreed to contribute a story, and Katherine mentioned his secretary, Gail Ledbetter, who agreed to help chronicle his life. Each chapter is the story told by the women who knew him. The stories are a combination of verbal interviews and letters written to me. I tried to maintain the narrative of the women as expressed to me. Their written accounts of Mr. Brown's life are as accurate as they can remember.

The women who told them to me approved each of the stories. There were omissions of some details because they were too personal; some details were added even though they were very personal. One of them didn't want her daughter to read the book until after she died. Another one said she might have been able to write a better story if she had the time. I didn't put to paper anything not approved by the women. All seemed very happy with this book.

Life Happens and I got married. It took me fifteen years to write this book between job and family.

Chapter 1
By Gail Ledbetter
(Jack's Secretary)

In the spring of 1960, Mr. Lloyd W. Sterling, the owner of Intricate Stamping Company (ISC), promoted me to personnel secretary on the condition that nothing of what I saw while working with the files ever left the office. "Not even your husband should know," he instructed me. This gave me the opportunity to be the first to meet and work with Jack Brown. His father had passed away that sweltering summer, and he took it upon himself to support the family.

He showed up for an application wearing his Sunday white shirt and a tie bought for him several years before. It was easy to see he had outgrown the tie at least a year ago. He was very confident for someone not yet eighteen years old; one could say he was brash. Sterling was passing the office as I explained to this adolescent applicant that ISC wasn't hiring. Jack said that he was dropping out of school to support his mother and siblings.

Sterling broke in and stated, "Under no circumstance are you to quit school."

Young Mr. Brown stood in awe of this dominant male. Sterling hired him, beginning immediately, and set the conditions for his employment: "Throughout the summer, you'll to report for work at 7 a.m. and work till 3:30 p.m., with a half-hour lunch in between. Starting the first day of school, you'll report to work directly after school. What time do you get out of class?"

"Three o'clock," the young man said with as much confidence as he could gather.

"You shall be here at three thirty, work till six thirty, go home and eat supper, do your homework, and go to bed. You'll report any Saturday that I need you. Starting wage is $2.50 an hour." This was strange because I had heard Sterling say in the past, "No teenager is worth minimum wage." Now he was paying this kid twice minimum wage.

"Well, John …," I began.

He interrupted me and said in a macho voice, "My friends call me Jack."

"Well, Jack," I said in my deepest voice, "looks like you found employment."

I was just twenty-five at that time, and my boyfriend, John, said I was quite the looker (John is my husband now, and he still says I'm quite the looker). I was very flattered and amused by the young man hitting on me.

With only two weeks of summer left, the production manager, Mr. Long, didn't want to train someone who wouldn't be working full-time. Joseph "Ol' Joe" Colachi, the maintenance supervisor, said he'd take the lad. Ol' Joe had earned his nickname because he had been with the company so long. He was only thirty-six when Jack was hired. I called him "Old Joe" one time, and he was quick to correct me. "Ol'" is a term of respect and admiration, but "old" is just old. Ol' Joe joined the army in 1941. That summer, he received a medical discharge after another soldier's gun jammed, and while freeing it, the gun misfired, striking Ol' Joe in the foot. That fateful December, he applied to the army again, but the army found out about his discharge and gave him a 4-F rating, keeping him out of the service.

I suspected this was where Ol' Joe got his disdain for officers and management. On several occasions, Sterling offered Ol' Joe a management position. He always replied, "Nobody will call me sir." If you watched him closely, he still had a limp in his step. Ol' Joe was a crusty man with a warm heart. Even though he was in the military for only a couple months, he cussed as if he spent his whole life there. He believed in getting his work done and done on time. On the other hand, he'd give you the shirt off his back if you needed it.

Every day at three thirty, when everyone else was heading home, Jack showed up for work. At first, Ol' Joe had him push a broom, but after a few weeks, Jack had worked out a system to do all the cleaning in just an hour.

I remember Ol' Joe complaining, "The cleaning should keep him busy and out of my hair."

After that, Ol' Joe started showing young Jack how to do minor maintenance. Jack caught on quickly and was soon helping with larger projects. One night, Joe and Jack worked on a machine until four in the morning. Sterling was quite upset with Joe keeping young Jack so late on a school night. Joe's defense was they completely rebuilt the power inverter. Sterling, who rarely acted surprised, was speechless at the accomplishment. In the past, they had to shut down for the whole day to rebuild the power converter.

In June 1961, Jack graduated from high school. One of the receivable clerks and a sorter in the plant had kids graduating at the same time. The word in the plant was the seniors were spending a weekend at the local amusement park after graduating. Ol' Joe asked Jack if he was going to join the other kids, and Jack replied he didn't have time for childish games. Ol' Joe pulled ten dollars out of his pocket and asked others to do the same. Before long, the entire mill raised over two hundred dollars for Jack to make the trip. They presented the money to him, but he still refused to go.

About this time, Sterling stopped by and heard what was happening. He called Jack into my office and stated, "After one year, everyone is entitled to a paid vacation. Your vacation starts the day after graduation and will go the entire week. When you return, you're to report Monday morning at seven o'clock. Since you'll be a full-time employee, the going rate for a maintenance person is three dollars an hour, retroactive today. If you show up the Monday after graduation, I will have security escort you from the premises." (We had no one in security.)

As on the first day, when Sterling spoke in this commanding manner, the awe-inspired Jack could only say, "Yes, sir."

Jack worked hard all summer, learning everything Ol' Joe could teach him. Jack came up with crazy ideas to improve the equipment or production line. Sterling would ask for something new, and Jack would give his idea. Ol'

Joe stared at the floor and chuckled if it was a bad idea, and he raised his right eyebrow if it was clever. The plant was having electrical problems. About once a week, it blew a fuse. One machine would continue while another stopped, causing a loss of product and time. Jack devised a plan to integrate the electric system. It would automatically shut down the whole line if one fuse blew, and none of the fuses would exceed 80 percent capacity. Ol' Joe checked with a friend who was an electrician and confirmed it was a great idea.

On a muggy August day in 1962, Ol' Joe and young Jack were finishing a project Jack had initiated. It was such a difficult project that Ol' Joe had looked at the floor and chuckled when he first heard it. Sterling's daughter, Sarah, showed up. She had just graduated from high school and was looking forward to college. She liked to pass through the mill to get to the offices. There was Jack, celebrating the completion of the project. He was swearing like a regular millwright in his tank top and blue jeans.

He pointed his finger at Ol' Joe and said, "Told you it could be done."

Sarah came through my office, which had a window to the mill. She stared through it for a moment. Then she turned to me and said, "He's awful full of himself, isn't he? Someone should take him down a peg." She went off to college without seeing Jack again.

In 1965, I was waiting to see Sterling when Ol' Joe showed up. It wasn't wise to get in Ol' Joe's way, so I let him go first. From the doorway, he told Sterling they would have to find a new assistant for him. "I'll need someone who will take my place someday," Ol' Joe explained.

"I thought it was Jack," said Sterling.

Ol' Joe smiled and replied, "No, Jack is replacing you." That was the extent of the conversation.

It was not but a month later that Sterling told me to change Jack from an hourly rate to salary plus commission. Jack was learning to be a salesperson. He read everything he could find on the subject. Since my office doubled as the company library, I checked out the books to Jack and even ordered new ones for him. His first assignment was to find companies that were no longer doing business with ISC and try to drum up the business again. It wasn't long before he was generating sales.

Sterling told him, "Any leads you generate in the field are yours."

Jack's bold blue eyes seemed to twinkle at the notion.

The next summer, Sarah returned from college. Jack now had a small corner office next to mine. Sarah stopped in his office and asked if he was just as conceited as he had been in the plant.

Jack said boldly, "It's not conceited if you can back it up."

She turned in a huff and walked away.

Later, Sterling asked me if I had heard what happened. I told him about the brief encounter, and he seemed somewhat pleased by the news, adding, "I love him like a son, but I don't think he's right for my daughter."

I heard they met at a nightclub in town a few nights later and started seeing each other. That winter, at the company Christmas party, a stumbling Jack grabbed the microphone and stopped the festivities. Everyone thought he was going to offer a toast for the holidays. Instead, he asked Sterling for his daughter's hand in marriage. Then he got on one knee and asked Sarah to marry him. I thought it was romantic, but Sarah stood up and yelled at him to shut up and get off the stage. Again, he asked her to marry him.

"Listen, you big dummy," she exclaimed, "If you're going to be the father of my children, you got to stop doing foolhardy stunts like this." Again, he asked her to marry him. She replied, "These people didn't gather to see my future husband make a fool of himself."

One more time, he asked, "Will you marry me?"

At this, Sterling stood up and said, "Tell the drunken fool yes so we can get on with the party."

The next June, they were married. I asked Sterling about Jack and Sarah; he remembered his comment from the year before and said, "When you're wrong, you're wrong. Now I'm worried about him. I have seen him stand up to guys twice his size, but when my daughter is strict, he looks like a deer in the headlamps."

They went on a monthlong honeymoon. One of the other salesperson said something about it, and Sterling pointed out Jack's last vacation had been in 1961.

The next few years were difficult for ISC. Most of the parts we produced went to the auto industry. The auto industry was changing; more and more car parts were made of plastic. Some parts were eliminated, and others were downsized. Even though Jack's sales were up, other sections of the company were failing miserably. Jack wanted to get into other industries, but Sterling was against it.

"All we know is auto work," he'd say. "To change is taking a terrible risk."

Jack offered to buy the company from Sterling. Even

with the declining sales, the company was worth a quarter-million dollars. Jack went to some bankers, got their backing, and raised the money to buy the company.

In September of 1972, Jack and Sarah became the official owners of Intricate Stamping Company. A couple months later, Sarah announced she was with child. Before the smiles had a chance to fade from everyone's faces, news came that Jack's younger brother died in Vietnam. A week later, his mother had a heart attack and passed away. His sister, who moved to California to get away from Jack and her mother controlling her life, didn't bother to come back for either funeral. Jack never showed it, but somehow this had a powerful and adverse effect on him. All I know is at age seventeen, his sister declared her independence and moved to California. Jack wanted to stop her, but his mother said it was futile because she'd be turning eighteen in a couple of months. She was only thirteen when her father died, and I think she resented him leaving her. The sister died a few years later from a drug overdose.

Ms. Stemple, who was Sterling's presidential secretary, retired when he left the company. Jack asked me to be his presidential secretary.

"What would I do?" I asked.

"Everything Ms. Stemple did for Mr. Sterling," he replied.

Several of the management staff retired or chose to take other positions when Jack took over. Two key people stayed on: Ol' Joe in maintenance and Long, manager of production. Jack felt he needed an engineer if they were going to stay in business and hired a young man by the name of Robert Owens.

Rob's old fraternity name was "Blockhouse." I never heard where he got this name, and he never used it in business. Rob was energetic and confident, but he didn't have a clue as to what he was getting into. We spoke one time about his fraternity. He said it was a black fraternity and really didn't help him when he got out of school.

Although he loved and admired his fraternity brothers, "if I had it to do over," he said, "I would have joined an established engineering fraternity."

Directly after Katherine was born, several large orders were canceled. Jack seized the opportunity and made a diligent search for new business. He went to a company in New England that manufactured water coolers. They required a part that would join an existing water line to a new heater system they had developed. Jack looked at their drawings and immediately remembered a part he and Ol' Joe fabricated for a machine they rebuilt when he was in high school.

He called me and asked me to remind Ol' Joe about the part and have him send it to him right away. "Use the new company that promises to get it here overnight," he said, referring to FedEx.

He arrived back the next night with some sketches and scribbled notes on scratch paper. The water company wanted a proposal on their desk by the end of the next week. Rob and Ol' Joe were there to meet him. I stayed with them until about 10 p.m. When I arrived the next morning, they were all asleep in Jack's office. They had a finished plan, but it would take more financing. Jack showered and left for the bank. He came back with the financing for 90 percent of the project. Sarah told him to take a second mortgage on the house.

The water company gave us an order for the part; ISC had six months to supply a trial run. The assembling of the new line didn't go as easily as first planned, and there were several cost overruns. The men had underestimated the power required to keep the line moving smoothly, and they needed an additional motor. Jack asked the management to forgo a paycheck, and he'd make it up to them. Only Rob and Ol' Joe agreed to the plan.

Money was still short. Ol' Joe knew Jack hadn't taken a paycheck in six months and mortgaged his house to 110 percent of value. Ol' Joe called on a contact he knew and got a deal on a new motor. With Ol' Joe's word to make good out of his own pocket, they would sell ISC a new motor on credit. They assembled the line in time for the trial run, and we supplied five hundred test pieces. They worked, and before long, we were into full production.

Shortly thereafter, we had a case of automotive parts returned for defects. This had never happened before. The truck arrived at nine in the morning, and Jack found out about it at ten. At eleven, he asked me to call a managers' meeting for one o'clock. It was ten after one when we arrived at the conference room. Mr. Long, his assistant, and the three floor supervisors were on one side of the table. Mr. Owens and our salesperson, Mr. Depew, were on the other. Ol' Joe was sitting in the corner, and a young machine operator was standing by the door.

Jack approached the young man at the door.

"Are you a manager?" he asked.

"No, sir," he replied.

"This is a managers' meeting," Jack said in a calm but stern voice. "You shouldn't be here."

"Mr. Long asked me to come," the young man answered.

Jack looked back for a moment and then said, "Why are you still here?"

With this, I heard a "Yes, sir," and out the door the young man scurried.

Jack went to the captain's chair at the head of the table and sat back while everyone bickered. He glanced back over his right shoulder to Ol' Joe and then turned his steel-blue eyes toward the table of men. One by one, the bickering stopped.

Jack stared at all of them for a moment more and then asked, "What's going on with this defective shipment?"

Long spoke up and started to explain why the parts failed, placing the fault on others.

Jack asked, "What's the status of these parts as we speak?"

Tony Pirelli, Long's new assistant, spoke up and said they were still on the dock, waiting instructions. At this, Jack turned to Harold Nixon, the newest supervisor.

"You're to get that box, open it, sort out the bad parts, replace them with good ones, box the shipment, and get it back to the customer tomorrow. You're to see to it personally. There are three test devices; employ them, and overtime is authorized."

Jack stared at the newest supervisor for a moment. "Why are you still here?" he asked.

"You meant now?" Harold murmured.

The reply was uncompromising: "From now on, all my commands are right now." (Jack later confided in me that he borrowed the line from a John Wayne movie.)

Jack then looked intently at Long and said, "If I ever have to do your job again, I will get someone else to do it. Mr. Long, make sure those parts ship tomorrow with 100 percent satisfaction. Now the problem is being corrected; how did it happen?"

Everyone just sat there, looking back at Jack as if he had the answer (knowing him, he probably did).

Jack peeked at Ol' Joe and asked, "Is it working?" (He was referring to the press machine in question.)

Ol' Joe snapped, "I don't have time to run it for them."

Jack said coldly, "Mr. Collins, you're named as foreman in charge on the production log."

Collins pointed out he was doing paperwork and was not actually on the floor.

Jack said, "Mr. Sommers, that leaves you in charge."

Sommers said he got the operator who made the parts but then noticed the operator was gone.

Jack said, "I sent him away; he's not management."

Sommers quipped, "Why did they send them back?"

Jack asked, "Mr. Depew, did you give any discounts for accepting defective parts?"

Depew said, "No."

Concise questions and short answers went on for about an hour. When Jack finished, the exact sequence of events that led to the defective parts was revealed. Furthermore, fault and blame were evenly distributed and accepted. Jack got everyone at the table to admit their fault, without accusing others. There was corrective action, so it wouldn't happen again.

I recognized the tone in his voice, which held all the men in the room fixated on his every word. It was the same voice young Jack used when I met him for the first time, in 1960. At age seventeen, it was a novice attempt at being firm, and it sounded brash. This was the first time I heard Jack speak this way as a leader. At no time did he ever raise his voice or use an expletive. He called everyone by his or her formal name for the whole hour. He was direct and cold. For me to listen to him in this mode was both exciting and frightening. No one spoke unless spoken to first. Jack had become the dominant male.

Sarah called toward the end of the meeting, and Jack stayed to speak with her. I left with the men and heard Rob say he grew up on the streets of Philadelphia during the riots, but nothing scared him as Jack did in that meeting.

When Jack got back to his office, he sent for Terrell Denkins, who usually ran the press the defective parts had been made on. He had gotten sick and went home at lunchtime that fateful day. Jack asked me and Karen Colvin, who took my place in personnel, to sit in on the meeting.

Terrell wasted no time in getting to Jack's office. Jack asked why he went home early on the day in question. Terrell said he had been ill.

"And you got better by the next day?" Jack asked.

Terrell admitted he was still sick when he showed up the next day. Jack explained the company policy on sickness to Terrell and asked if he was aware of it. Terrell answer in the affirmative.

Jack issued a formal verbal warning to Terrell for coming in sick. "If you're legitimately sick, I don't want you infecting the other employees. If you're hung over, I expect you to come to work and suffer through it. Now that finishes my work as president; as owner of the company, I'm pleased you thought so highly of us to come in while you were sick. Since work is twice as hard when sick, I'm paying double time for the entire week."

Karen interjected that the checks were already made up for the week.

"The checks are not distributed until tomorrow," he said. "We have time to change it."

Terrell made a point of shaking Jack's hand before leaving.

The next Monday, Jack decided it was a good idea for us to make weekly strolls through the plant, as he used to do. We stopped by to see Terrell and asked how he was doing. Terrell stated he'd be doing a lot better if all white men were like Jack. He went on to explain that with the added money in his check last week, his wife and he had the down payment on a house, but the bank wouldn't loan them the money. Jack asked which bank they used. It was a statewide bank in town. Jack gave him the name of a person at the local bank where we did business.

The next morning, Terrell showed up at Jack's office. Jack said he always had time for Terrell. He thanked Jack for getting him the loan.

"I didn't do anything but point you in the right direction" Jack replied.

Terrell explained he met with the loan officer at four o'clock, and by five, he had the loan on the condition his credit history checked out. The bank would have the final papers ready in a couple weeks.

Jack looked at Terrell as he was leaving and said, "Right is right, and wrong is wrong. Wrong is neither white nor black; it is just wrong. A person who is wrong cannot even be called a man. You have always done right by me, and I have tried to do right by you."

Terrell answered, "Yes, sir," and then looked Jack in the eyes and repeated, "Yes, sir."

I missed the point that Jack was making until I met with Terrell about a month after Jack passed away. Terrell just had his first grandbaby, and he was a cutie. To see Terrell's chest stuck out, you would think he personally built the BP Building. Within a couple minutes of this chance encounter, we were having a cup of coffee and reminiscing about Jack. He asked me if I remembered the meeting in his office, and of course I had. What Jack said to him as he was leaving made quite an impression. Terrell raised his children to know "right is right and wrong is wrong." I asked what he meant by that, and Terrell explained that when he was a boy, his momma would tell him that two wrongs didn't make a right. When Terrell said all white men should be like Mr. Brown, he was as wrong as the banker who denied him the loan for being black. I remembered thinking he was profound for someone who had dropped out of high school.

In the twenty years I worked for Jack, there was only one time he was sick. It was in the early eighties, and he showed up at the office one Monday a little after eight o'clock. He walked by me and barely said hello. Ten minutes later, Sarah was on the phone, looking for that husband of hers. I hesitantly said he was in his office.

"Oh, is he?" she cried out.

Jack and Sarah lived about ten minutes from the plant; it took her all of five minutes to get here, with a stop at

Rob's office. She stormed into Jack's office and couple of minutes later came out with him in tow. Jack had that "deer in headlamps" look Sterling mention so many years before.

Rob showed up, and Sarah told him, "You're in charge for the rest of the week. Mr. Brown won't be in the office. I will call you to let you know when you can drop his car off to him."

Jack glanced at Rob as if to say, "Save me"; Rob said sarcastically, "*You* made her CEO."

Sarah was the only person who had a stronger will than Jack. I called her during the week, and she said, "He's being a big baby. On Monday, Jack sent me out to get cough syrup, and before I could get out of the drive, he escaped to the office. This whole week, he's had a 102 fever. He will cough up mucus and then announce he's feeling better and should go to the office the next day. He won't stay in bed, won't admit he's sick, and it's taking everything I have to keep him down."

I got the impression that when Sarah was irritated, Jack's charm and charisma had no effect on her. When Jack got full of himself, Sarah was the one to bring him down a peg.

Jack was a charmer. I remember a time in the late eighties, three young women came from a nearby college. They were all part of a sorority for women in business. They wanted Jack to give a speech at the college. We all met in his office for an hour, and he agreed to the speech. He spent the whole hour telling jokes and anecdotes about himself and the company. After the women left, I mentioned he was flirting with them.

"Those young girls? I'm old enough to be their father," Jack proclaimed.

I replied that if he asked them to remove their clothing, they probably would have done so. Jack rolled his eyes at me in disbelief.

The eighties were good for ISC. We doubled the plant size, tripled the work force, and added a few managers while quadrupling the number of parts to person-hours worked. Jack was interested in hiring a woman manager after the meeting with the women in the business sorority. He had me send job requests to all the usual locations and told me to send one to the girl's sorority on that campus and at a couple more colleges. One of the graduates who sent us a resume had visited us the year before. Jack was impressed with her qualifications. She had good grades and worked as a manager in a restaurant. I called her for an interview. After the interview, Jack wanted to hire her but said we probably wouldn't get her, as she was looking more for a banker's position than a manufacturing.

"Banking is more glamorous than this," he said, referring to the dusty plant.

I called her back for a second interview a week later; she stated exactly what he had predicted.

In 1988, Rob was promoted to vice president of sales and marketing. This was the first time ISC had a vice president. I asked Jack if he was grooming Rob to take over someday.

"I don't groom anyone," he said. "They groom themselves."

I asked about Mr. Long, who had been at ISC for quite a while.

"Mr. Long has been content to stay the manager of production," he said. "He's a very good manager of production." He added that Mr. Long viewed sales as a waste of time and money, as if new orders grew on trees and could be picked at any time. Maintenance was to stay out of sight until required and then fix problems in the blink of an eye.

Jack went on to say Rob had learned all facets of the company. He started in production, he helped with maintenance, and when asked, he did a superb job at sales. He also kept up on OSHA, EPA, and IRS laws and protocols.

"Rob has always been there when I needed him," he said. "A good manager doesn't have to pick an employee for promotion; the employee steps forward."

Soon after Rob became VP, Peter Kerry Jr., the president of a competitor, the now-defunct Kerry Parts Company, wanted to buy parts from us. They were making their own parts and looking to outsource the work. Jack told Kerry that Rob would make the arrangements. Kerry said he didn't like working with black people (only he used a derogatory term).

Jack said coldly, "We really don't have the capacity to handle any more business." The man started to say something, but Jack said sternly, "Good day."

After the "gentleman" left, Rob challenged Jack by saying, "I thought it was you who said not to let your personal feeling get in the way of business"

Jack started to say something, paused, and said okay, adding, "If you can get the business, you can have it. Be sure to get a premium because we will be using old equipment and pushing overtime."

Rob struck up a deal with the Kerry Company, and we made three monthly shipments. Payment was slow for the first three shipments, and we held the fourth until we received a check. Jack received a call from the Kerry Company and had me conference with Rob. They didn't have the money to send us but needed that fourth shipment. They asked if we would be willing to discount the shipment to get it off our docks. Jack emphatically said no.

Immediately after the phone call, Rob was waiting to see Jack. Jack asked me to take notes. Rob was curious as to how Jack knew this was going to happen.

Jack explained, "Sometimes, you should trust the hairs on the back of your neck. I have known of Mr. Kerry for ten years now, and this only cements his unscrupulous reputation."

Rob asked what would happen to the parts. Jack smiled and pointed out that with the deal Rob made, the first two checks covered our cost on the parts, and we could afford to dump the fourth shipment on the open market.

As 1989 started, Ol' Joe was talking about retirement. He said it was getting old being there every day. All the machines were computerized, and his skills hadn't kept up. Jack asked me what he should do. I couldn't imagine Ol' Joe retiring, even though he was soon to be sixty-five years old.

"Ol' Joe has worked for this company nearly forty-eight years," he said. "What do you get a guy who's served that long?"

I mentioned that a gold watch is traditional.

In February 1989, Ol' Joe turned sixty-five and announced his retirement. Jack called him into his office and said he wouldn't know what to do without him; he offered to pay him $100 per week as a consultant. This left the door open for Ol' Joe to come back whenever he felt like it. Jack confided that everyone but Ol' Joe had pulled out of the company pension plan. With the modern times, the others had opted for a 401(k) plan. Everything left in the old plan must belong to him. Ol' Joe wasn't hot or cold about the pension until he asked how much. Jack had me read the amount.

"Something is wrong," the newly retired man said excitedly. "I can't take two hundred thousand dollars."

Jack piped up, "No one else can; it has your name on it. If I take it, I can go to jail."

Ol' Joe just mumbled something.

Jack came back with "For that much money, you'd think I could call you sir one time?"

Ol' Joe just gave a daring stare to Jack.

A couple of nights later, we had a dinner for Ol' Joe's retirement. Jack presented Ol' Joe with a gold Rolex with eleven diamond points marking eleven of the hours and a big diamond for the twelfth hour. Jack added, "In 1973, you loaned me money by not taking a paycheck. Now that you're retiring, it is time to repay you that loan; with interest, that comes out to be ten thousand dollars." Jack told me that night, "Ol' Joe will take a week, maybe two, and he will be back."

He did come back on a part-time basis, coming and going as he pleased, but he always took Wednesdays off for golf.

Jack continued to groom Rob to take over someday. In the spring of 1991, there were many closed-door meetings between them. Around the first of May, Jack asked me about my John. Jack had heard he was looking to retire. My John's sixtieth birthday was coming, and he wanted to retire early and do some traveling. Jack said Katherine was graduating this year, and he and Sarah were looking forward to a vacation. He was thinking a weekend in Vegas; Sarah was thinking world cruise. We discussed my future, and Jack hinted of many changes in June.

On Monday in the second week of May, Sarah asked Jack to take her to the doctor's office. Jack joked it was either menopause or she was pregnant. Sarah had been feeling rundown for a while and wanted to get it checked out. They were gone the entire day. On Wednesday, the doctor called and wanted to see both Jack and Sarah in his office. "This morning," Jack repeated. He half-heartedly joked that she must be pregnant. I don't think he was prepared to hear what the doctor said. Later that day, when Rob had a problem and asked me to call Jack, before I could describe the work dilemma, Jack told me, "Have Rob handle it," in a crackled voice. We didn't hear from him the rest of the week, and no one dared to call him.

We all knew something was wrong, but no one could have guessed what we heard on the following Monday. Jack called me at lunchtime to set up a manager's meeting at four thirty. A lifeless Jack straggled in at four o'clock and met behind closed doors with Rob. He didn't even look at me when he passed. At four thirty, the two came out and started for the conference room. Jack turned to me and quietly asked if I would join them. Rob's eyes were red and swollen, and his chin, which was usually high, had dropped to his chest.

The three of us arrived at the conference room, and Jack made a point to seat Rob in the captain's chair. He announced in the best voice he could muster, "Rob is president pro tem until further notice. Company bylaws require the president to be stockholder in the company. Many years ago, Rob loaned the company money by forgoing a check at a critical time. It is time I repaid him. By signing this document, Rob will own a total of 25 percent of Intricate Stamping Company."

With his hands shaking, Rob took the pen from Jack, and we all watch him sign his name. It was so quiet in the room; you could hear the pen scratching the paper as Rob signed his name several times.

Jack took the paperwork, gave a copy to Rob, and put the rest in his jacket pocket. He stood there for a moment to gather himself. His hands were clamped together tight. The veins on the back of his hands were bulging. Knuckles and fingertips were a blistering red and white from the pressure. I looked at his neck, and his Adam's apple was pulsating like a gobbling turkey neck. His face was drawn and without expression. For the first time in thirty years, he couldn't find the words. He started to speak, stammered, coughed, and started again in a slow and distinct manor, coercing each word out his month and a crackle in each vowel:

"I'm forced to take a leave of absence, effective today. Rob will be in charge and have full authority in all aspects of Intricate Stamping Company. Last Wednesday, Sarah and I found out cancer has ravaged her body, and she has six months to a year to live, and I plan to be with her the entire time."

Jack swiftly left the room, touching my arm on the way out. I looked around at everyone. About twenty men and five women were fighting back tears. Long had buried his head in his elbow on the table. I could see his shoulders flexing up as he tried to hold his emotions. Rob sat uneasily in the captain's chair. Red eyes and welled-up faces were all around me. I just stood there, watching everyone; I wasn't crying, wasn't upset, and felt very, very cold inside. The next thing I knew, Karen Colvin was wiping my eyes with a Kleenex, and Tony was sliding a chair underneath me. Rob came over to me and held my hand. He was saying something, but all I could hear were Jack's shattered words passing repeatedly through my head. Rob called my John to come pick me up. As I was leaving, I noticed a few spouses had come to pick up their loved ones.

The next day, there were abundant rumors concerning the meeting the day before and what was wrong with Jack. I was worried about Ol' Joe; I didn't want him hearing the news from anyone else, so I called him at home. He said Jack called last Thursday and told him what had happened. Ol' Joe said he wouldn't be in that afternoon. I mentioned the rumors to Rob and said that the employees were wondering about the status of ISC. Rob asked Tony to shut everything down and gather the employees. Rob tried his best to explain what Jack had conveyed the afternoon before. He choked up as the words came out of his mouth. Long had to finish for Rob. Almost everyone present had teary eyes.

The following Monday morning, Jack brought Sarah for a last visit. She sat in Jack's office and let everyone come to see her. She had to agree to these conditions before Jack would let her visit. She was in good spirits. Jack wanted to know why Rob hadn't remodeled the president's office. Rob shrugged his shoulders.

Jack said, "We've been planning a change for June. You know what to do." He gathered up a few mementos and told Rob, "Bring anything that doesn't fit to the house."

After the office staff had visited Sarah, one special person came from the shop. Ol' Joe peeked his head in the door and asked if it was okay for him to enter.

Sarah wanted to know why he hadn't called on her at the house, and Ol' Joe responded, "This is a time for family."

She gave him a puppy dog look and said, "You powdered my behind; if that's not family, what is?"

Ol' Joe's demeanor softened. Jack left the two alone.

After a while, at the behest of Sarah, Ol' Joe announced to Jack (who thought he was in charge), "I'm going to carry Sarah to the plant."

Jack drew a deep breath, held it, and then sighed. (He was outnumbered.) He agreed to let her go to the plant and sit in a chair so everyone could come say hi. Ol' Joe had some of the workers carry a big comfortable lounge chair from the foyer out to the shop. Jack took Sarah's arm and led her to the plant. All the workers lined up to greet her. Ol' Joe kept the line moving. The very last person through the line was Terrell. He tried to say hi, but only tears came out. No one else touched her, but when Sarah saw Terrell crying, she reached up and grabbed his trembling hand and held it.

She joked, "Big macho types are all the same: tough as a cookie on the outside and marshmallow on the inside."

Jack and Rob were talking quietly off to the side. Tony asked Ol' Joe to help him with one of the machines, and this left me watching over Sarah. This was her moment alone with the plant. She gazed all around with wonder in her eyes. In that moment, I could see in her face the little girl in pigtails trying to keep up with Daddy; the teenager spying a strong young man celebrating a success; and the back wall torn down to double the size of the plant. For the first time that day, she had tears in her eyes and looked tired.

When we got back to the offices, Jack pulled me into his old office and told me he might not come back to work, and Rob wanted me to help him for a couple of months so he could be acclimated to the new job. After that, I would have the choice of retiring or finding another position.

I told Jack my John was retiring in a couple of months, and we were planning to travel.

"Please stay with him until then," he said.

After Jack and Sarah left, Rob had Long come into his office. He said, "As of today, you are vice president. Get down to your office, clean it out, and move everything into my old office. What do you think of having Tony take your job?" Long commented he didn't think Rob and Tony saw eye to eye. "We don't, but that doesn't mean he's not a good man," replied Rob.

Rob went around making the changes as discussed with Jack. Karen officially became personnel manager, an easy move, as she had always attended management meetings. We completed our rounds of the office. Rob asked me who was ready for a full-time secretary's job, and I suggested Elane in payroll. We stopped and talked to Elane, and she agreed to become a full-time secretary. We all went to Tony's office, which was no more than a cubical in the plant.

Rob looked at Tony and said, "I am the new president; clear your desk out." Tony's face went blank. After pausing for a moment, Rob continued, "Elane is your new secretary, and she will help you move into your new office."

It was the first week of June before I stopped to see Jack and Sarah at home. Sarah was looking good, but Jack was losing the middle age bulge from around his waist. Noticing a vial of painkillers, I asked Sarah if she was in pain. She said no, although I saw her wince a couple of times while visiting. I stayed for about an hour; Katherine joined us for a little while. I came out of Sarah's room, and Jack was sleeping on a couch just outside her door. Sarah had advised me not to wake him, since he hadn't been sleeping well.

It was August; Sarah was looking very thin and had an IV connected to her hand. She looked as if she lost twenty pounds; Jack must have lost thirty to forty pounds. Katherine came into the room and asked if I could get her dad to eat.

"I will send Ol' Joe," I said. "He'll make your dad eat."

Ol' Joe stopped to see me a couple days later. He had gotten Jack to eat and even leave the house for a while. After that, Ol' Joe, Rob, and I took turns meeting with Jack; we encouraged him to eat and get out for a while. This made Sarah happy.

On September 4, I stopped to see Sarah and take Jack out to eat, but he wouldn't leave her side. She was awake and alert, and seemed in good spirits for her frail condition.

Jack called me at home later that day, and all he could say was, "It's over."

Ol' Joe handled the details of Sarah's funeral. He even got Sterling to come to the funeral. On Jack's forty-eighth birthday, Sarah was laid to rest.

My John and I had Jack over for dinner at least once a week after that. As we approached the holidays, I noticed Jack getting a little depressed. He tried to show a brave front, but from time to time, you could see the anxiety. Katherine was getting ready for college. She had skipped the first quarter with her mother's passing away. I looked at Jack and suggested he go to college. He looked at me as if I suggested he go to the moon. Then he smiled and said he might do that.

Jack got Katherine off to school in January. My John and I saw less and less of him as time went on. I realized Jack hadn't been to church since Sarah's diagnosis with cancer. I invited him to church, and he smiled and said it wasn't time yet. In June of that year, he asked me to help him get into college, since it was my idea. He had mentioned on a regular basis that his only regret was not being able to get a college education, but now it was my idea. He registered at a local college and started classes in the fall, a year after Sarah passed away. I noticed he had regained most of the weight he lost when caring for Sarah. I knew he'd be all right.

Jack always stayed in touch with us. Sometimes, it was difficult due to the traveling we were doing and the schedule Jack kept. He got involved in civic organizations to help the community.

I asked him to go with us on a trip, and he simply said, "There is nothing finer out there than what I can find in this town."

I think it was Sarah's memory that kept him close to home. I checked in on ISC occasionally. Rob was taking the company to new places, and Jack was counseling him on a regular basis. The company got completely out of the automotive industry.

About two years before Jack passed a way, he started back to church. In his younger days, he was very somber at church. Recently, I noticed him crying and being more vocal during the service.

My John and I left for Florida a day after Easter in April 2002. We were enjoying the sunshine and company of some friends we met on our travels. They owned a condominium in the Keys, and we rented a unit from their association. We had been there ten days when we got a call from our daughter, telling us that Jack passed away. I dropped the phone when I heard the news. My John and I caught the next plane for Ohio.

Jack was a good boss and a better friend to me. If I were to cheat on my John, it would have been with Jack. I can say this without my John getting jealous because what attracted me to Jack was the very thing that would keep us apart. Jack was probably the last of the men who truly kept their word. If Jack told you that he'd do something, it was done. When he committed to Sarah, it was nonnegotiable.

In the mid-eighties, my John and I were having problems. I went to Jack for comfort. Instead, he gave me some much-needed advice. He pointed out when other couples reached this point in life, the wife tended to baby the husband, and they were not used to the attention. He also pointed out that husbands didn't always see the changing interests of their wives. Men should see these changes, but men can be thick-headed. He suggested I speak to John like a wife and not a mother. Jack always seemed to know what to say and do in every situation. It wasn't so much what he said but how he said it that made the difference.

I will miss Jack, and so will my John. The only other time I saw him cry was when his father died. This community is less than what it was, now that Jack is gone. Rob put a memorial in the lobby of Intricate Stamping Company. It listed the past two presidents, with Jack's name in gold.

Chapter 2
By Katherine Brown Williams
(Jack's Daughter)

John "Jack" Brown was my dad. I have always called him Dad and will remember him as Dad. Fathers can be anything, but Dads are always loving, tender, and sensitive, even when they are angry with you. No matter how angry Dad got or how much I disappointed him, a simple "Luv ya" would calm him down. A simple smile from him would pick me up from my doldrums. His smile was infectious. His love for Mom and me was genuine.

My first real memory of my dad was when I was four years old. He went away for a week, and I missed him terribly. Mom tried to comfort me while he was gone, but it was his phone calls every night that helped me through the week. He came home on Thursday from his trip. I still like to think it was for me alone. Until I was sixteen, every Christmas, Mom and I would have to stay at the top steps and wait for him to set up Christmas. He'd plug in the lights on the tree and turn on the movie camera. He always got a shot of Mom and me parading down the steps and into the family room. He'd place the camera on a tripod and tape everyone enjoying the events of that glorious morning.

When I was eight years old, Mom got me in soccer. It was a league in town. There were six teams in the league. Our coach was Ms. White. I remember her saying winning wasn't important; it was how we play the game. We lost our first four games, and I wanted to quit.

Dad said, "The Browns don't quit something they started."

The next practice, Dad and I showed up, and all the other kids had their uniforms in a pile. Everyone was quitting. Dad said this would set a bad example. Ms. White didn't know why everyone quitting. It turned out that winning was important; it was the reason for me to quit. Dad asked Ms. White why we were not winning, and a disgruntled Ms. White told him he didn't understand little kids.

Dad stared at Ms. White and coldly stated, "I understand my daughter's quitting because she hates losing."

When other fathers got angry, they would scream and yell. When Dad got mad, he turned cold and spoke calmly but sternly. My girlfriends said this scared them more than their fathers yelling.

Ms. White turned white at Dad's comment. She said, "If you can do better, then you coach."

Dad turned to my teammates and asked if they would play if there was a chance of winning. All but one girl said yes (I don't think she liked the game, anyhow). Dad coached our soccer team for the next three years. That year we went five and five the rest of the season. The next year, we won all but two games and were champions. The last year, we were undefeated and beat the all-boy team twice.

For the most part, Dad was like a big lion you see on television. If everything was going well, then he was calm and playful. Mom would handle punishing me. When things got very bad, then Dad would be the one to punish me. I could argue with Mom, especially in my teenage years, but with Dad, there was no arguing. He'd sit me down and ask me questions about the offence I committed. He expected quick and truthful responses.

I remember playing with a toy, and Dad asked me a question in his mad voice; without thinking, I told him something that was untrue. He stomped on my toy and asked me if I'd like to lose another toy. I told him the truth and never lied to him again. The one thing my dad didn't like was to have anyone lie to him. He grounded me for a week for what I did; I lost a toy and missed a girlfriend's birthday party for lying to him.

I had my first boyfriend when I was twelve. It lasted Thursday and Friday. Saturday morning, my friend Susie Drennan called and said she heard the boy liked someone else. After making a few more calls, I learned the devastating news was true. My world came crashing down all around me. I went looking for Mom. She had gone shopping. Dad asked what was wrong. I burst into tears and ran into my bedroom.

Dad followed me. He again asked, "What's wrong?" and I sobbed, "Where's Mom?"

"Your mother is out and won't be back for a while," he replied. He stood there for a moment with a puzzled look on his face. "Is it female problems?"

I tried my best to explain what had happened that morning. He asked if I had kissed the boy. No, I rumbled at him.

"Good," Dad joked. "I would have made you marry him if you had kissed him."

I looked at him, and the corners of his mouth were slightly turned up. Then he smiled at me. I couldn't help but smile back at him. When he smiled, even his eyes were smiling at you. We talked for an hour about boys. He informed me that boys were ignorant and didn't become interested in girls for another year. Until they grew up, he added, they were fickle about girls.

When Mom got home later that day, we spoke about what happened that morning. She told me I scared Dad by the outburst that morning. I wanted to talk with her about boys, but instead, we talked mostly about her and Dad. Between what Mom and Dad said, it all seemed to make sense. I got over the boy, and by Monday, there was a new boy to break my heart. I found out that enlightened Saturday there were no subjects I couldn't broach to my parents (with maybe the exception of female problems with Dad).

In the fall of 1985, I started junior high; algebra was the required math. The problems in the book were hard for me to understand. I went to Mom and asked her for help; she had the college degree. She said her degree was in political science, and math wasn't her strength (I guess I inherited her math skills). I would much rather have Mom help me with homework than Dad. Mom would give me some answers, help me figure others, and then leave me on my own. Dad, on the other hand, wanted me to figure it all by myself. I admit that I learned more with Dad than with Mom. It seemed every night, there was Dad, helping me with my homework, never giving me the answer but always pointing in the right direction. By the end of the school year, I really didn't need his help anymore, but it made him feel good to help me.

Before eighth grade, I needed to go clothes shopping. Mom wasn't feeling well and said Dad would take me shopping. I don't think Mom knew, but I needed underwear. We went to the teen section of the department store in town. We were looking at dresses, pants, and shirts. Most of what Dad held up was nice, but I laughed off a few.

He held up one loud dress and said, "You'll look just like Grandma." We both laughed.

After a while, I told him what I needed. He stood there for a moment with a perplexed look on his face. It was obvious he wasn't ready to go underwear shopping with his daughter. For a second, I thought he was going to make an excuse to get out of it.

With a half-hearted grin, he said, "Let's go see what they have."

The first thing he picked up was a training bra. He started to say, "This is a nice one," then he noticed I already had boobs. Mom was average size upstairs, but by age thirteen, I was bigger than she was. I don't think he noticed how developed I was until that very moment. It became clear by the time we reached the women's section; he was uncomfortable helping me find a bra. Sweat was forming on his forehead, but he tried his best to help me. I jokingly asked him if I should try one on and show it to him. He just glared at me. I laughed, and he tried to laugh.

I saw a thong on display and thought about asking for it, but I figured he'd pass out at that point.

When we got home, Dad took some aspirin and went to bed. As soon as he was out of sight, whatever was ailing Mom seemed to go away.

"Let us see what you bought," she announced.

I opened the bag and showed her the bras and panties that I purchased.

She cried out, "I thought you were buying clothes." She explained that Dad said he knew his daughter and would be able to pick out clothes she'd like.

I told Mom how embarrassed Dad was picking out bras for me. I emphasized, "Dad stuck to the end and asked the right questions about size and style. I would've been embarrassed, if it wasn't for his embarrassment."

In Dad's defense, I let Mom know he had picked out clothes that I liked and would wear.

A few weeks later, Dad was dropping me off at school. Occasionally, he liked to drive me in the morning so we could talk. We only lived about ten minutes from school, but it always took us a half-hour to get there when he drove. That morning, he asked how I was adjusting to school.

When I was getting out of the car, he said the usual: "Luv ya."

Some other girls heard him say it and gave me a tough time all day. The next day, he made it a point to drive me to school again. We arrived early. When I got out, he said, "L-Y." I knew what he meant.

In 1989, I had my sixteenth birthday. I was looking forward to getting my license to drive. Dad announced driving was a man's domain, and he'd teach me to drive. This made me feel better. It wasn't his antiquated outburst; Mom's driving scared me. She was very talented in many things, but driving wasn't one of them. I think it must do with the changing times. When she was a girl, women didn't drive much. Driving was a man's thing; now, girls drive as much as the boys do.

Dad took me out three or four times for training runs through empty parking lots. I had to learn how to parallel park, even though it wasn't required on the driving test. When he took me out on city streets for the first time, it didn't take long before I was comfortable behind the wheel. Driving was fun. I asked Dad when he was going to get me my own car. He replied that I'd get a new car at the same age my grandfather got my mother her own car.

We got home, and in my excitement, I mentioned Dad was getting me my own car. Mom had a puzzled look on her face and asked if he really said that.

I told her, "He said he'd buy me a car at the same age Grandpa bought you your first car."

Mom explained with a smile on her face, "To this point, your grandpa has never bought me a car."

Dad was a man of his word; I knew if I wanted a car, I must get a job. I still think it was a dirty trick. I cannot wait to do it to my kids.

In my junior year, I spent a night over Susie's house. Mom and Dad thought Susie's parents were to be home that night. As it turned out, they got tickets to a show in Cleveland and left the two us home alone. We were not expecting her parents back until well after midnight. We got the bright idea to sneak into her dad's liquor cabinet.

We carefully poured a drink into a couple of tall glasses and filled the bottle with water back to the original volume. After the third drink, we forgot to add water back into the bottle. We were sitting down and enjoying our first taste of adulthood when the front door opened, and her parents exploded at the sight of two sixteen-year-old girls having a nightcap at their expense.

The father was yelling; the mother was screaming. For the first time, I knew the difference. Susie's dad phoned my dad and informed him of the evening events. Susie lived two houses away from us. I watched the clock on the wall, waiting for Dad to come get me. I've heard of time standing still, and at that very moment, I realized it could happen. The second hand would stop for an eternity before moving to the next second. It took exactly two minutes and thirty-two seconds for Dad to get dressed and come get me. It seemed like a lifetime. I started picturing myself at a military school or maybe a convent. In the past, Dad said I didn't know what it was like to be in the doghouse. I even pictured myself having to live the rest of my days in a doghouse in the backyard. Between the alcohol, the lateness of the hour, and the fear of my parents and what they would say, I was terrified.

I heard the knock on the door, which meant it was Dad (Mom wouldn't have knocked). Between Mom and Dad, I thought Dad was less likely to kill me on the way home. Dad shook Mr. Drennan's hand, looked at me, and said, "Let's go." He didn't say a word all the way home. The pace he set was quite fast for me in my condition. Somehow, I knew not to say anything.

We got home, and Mom wanted to know what had happened. Dad said, "Smell her breath."

Mom got about a foot away and yelled in a shrill voice I had never heard before, "What in Hades have you been doing?"

I never heard Mom swear. Dad would cuss when in the garage or at work, but never Mom.

I muttered, "We had a drink."

Mom screeched back, "A drink? You smell like a distillery. Get upstairs. We'll see you in a little bit."

It seemed a half-hour passed, and I was having trouble keeping my eyes open. Dad showed up at the door and then realized I wasn't ready for bed, and fear came over me again. He stood there for a moment, turned, and walked away. I hurriedly changed into my pajamas and waited awhile longer.

Mom came up to my room and said, "You changed; we'll see you in the morning."

It was 4 a.m. when I woke from my inebriated slumber. It was just after midnight when Mom said she'd see me in the morning. For the first time that night, things were clear in my head as to what I had done and my parents' reaction to it. I realized Mom had cussed at me; she was madder than ever before. Not even Dad could make her mad enough to cuss, but I did. Then I thought about Dad. He wasn't angry; he seemed more upset, disappointed, and hurt by my actions the night before. It was about that time I could hear the television downstairs.

I went to investigate. There was Dad, sitting glassy-eyed in front of the TV, switching channels, without watching any of them. He skimmed through one by one until it started over. I moved so he could more easily see me; the channels kept changing. Dead silence was something I

DANIEL MACPHERSON

never experience from him before. He wouldn't even make eye contact.

I moved directly in front of him, smiled, and said, "Luv ya."

With this, he raised his right arm for me to crawl under. I snuggled next to him, as I did when I was a small child. We sat there for a moment; I felt him hold me tight around the shoulders. Then his arm moved up and clinched around my head, and with the point of his hard knuckles, he gave me some nuggies atop my head. He often did this to me when I was younger and did something foolish, until Mom caught him one day and told him to never do it again.

My head was throbbing but didn't hurt. He asked me what I was thinking the night before. Normally, Dad would expect short answers to his questions, and I knew at this moment complete honesty was of utmost importance. I also knew "I don't know" would get me more nuggies. I explained that Susie and I thought it would be cool if we tried a drink. We were on our third when Mr. and Mrs. Drennan came home. I did my best to explain everything that led up to us pouring out those wicked solutions.

He explained that the booze was an inanimate object, which was neither good nor bad. For something to be good or bad, it must have a soul and have eaten from the tree of good and evil.

I replied, "Sixteen-year-old girls know that drinking is evil; therefore, I'm evil for drinking."

"Not quite," he said. "What you did was wrong, but you're not evil. Everybody is a sinner. There has been only one perfect man on this earth; everyone else has sinned. Realizing your actions were wrong, taking steps to correct the situation, and trying not to do it again makes you good."

"So does this mean I'm not grounded?" I asked, smiling at him.

He gave me a look that said "You better be joking" and replied, "A week of grounding and a month without your license." He paused and added, "If your story checks out with the Drennans, you may go to the dance on Friday." Shock must have run over my face because he added, "You thought I forgot about that."

I asked why he was so upset, and he looked at me as if I was daft. I qualified my question by saying, "You're still up at this hour."

"Firstly," he stated, "what do you say the first time you catch your sixteen-year-old drinking? I didn't know what to say. When I was younger, I had nights where I put away a few drinks. It is easy to lose control when you're young and drinking. Sometime in your life, you must realize if you don't control your drinking, then it will control you. Secondly, what you did to your mother has me in a quandary. I've never seen her so upset, and trust me when I say, I've tried in the past to get her that mad."

I said, "I thought Mom wanted to give me nuggies with a club last night."

The next morning, Dad woke me up at seven o'clock, stating if I was going to drink like a grown-up, I'd have to pay the price as a grown-up. I didn't know what he meant until I tried to move. Something was tugging on my head. I thought my hair was caught on something, but no: It was just my head, not wanting to move. It took a while for me to come downstairs. Dad had breakfast on the table for me. Pancakes, sausage, toast, and eggs were spread out on the table.

Mom and Dad were in a heated discussion before I made it to the kitchen. Dad announced a good breakfast was required after the night I had. I sat down at the table, and he pushed the food under my nose. Normally, it was an honor to receive this attention from Dad. The aroma wafted over me, and my stomach started doing flip-flops. I was trying to eat when I looked up at Dad. He was nudging Mom and smiling. He seemed to get immense joy out of seeing me suffer. I must have looked pitiful because Mom, who hadn't said two words to me all morning, looked at me and started laughing too. She asked if I'd like some coffee. I wondered where the clearness I felt at 4 a.m. had gone. Now there was a fuzzy buzzing in my head.

I was hoping to stay home from church, but Dad said, "Nothing doing."

By the time we made it to church, the buzzing in my head turned to a headache, and thoughts of sleeping filled my mind. The preacher was especially loud that morning. Each word seemed to resonate in my head, and when the preacher was resolute, my whole body flexed. After church, Mom was going to let me sleep, but Dad said this was all part of my punishment and gave me some chores to do. By three o'clock that afternoon, I was wishing for parents who would beat me silly instead of going through Dad's punishment.

About eight o'clock that night, Mom snuck me some aspirin, and I was starting to feel a little better. They were on the couch discussing me, as if I already went to bed.

Mom was thinking my escapades from the night before should preclude me from going to the dance on Friday. Dad explained my story rang true with Drennans, and for being honest about what happened, he thought I should go. They compromised: I could go, and Dad would drive me there at eight and pick me up at ten thirty when it was over. Mom admitted Dad's punishment was more suited than what she had in mind.

Dad replied, "You may know your daughter better than me, but I know the effects of drinking better than you."

I never did find out what Mom had in store for me, but it couldn't have been worse than what Dad did to me.

High school went by fast. Boys came, and boys went. My heart was never broken the way the first boy broke it. It didn't matter who the boy was; if he was to take me out, he had to meet Dad first. I started dating Mike Utica in late October my senior year. When he came to pick me up, Dad, Ol' Uncle Joe, and Uncle Terrell were in the den. I felt bad that Mike had to deal with the three of them, but Mom was holding me up. By the time I got downstairs, Mike was waiting by the door. We went to dinner and a movie. The whole night, there wasn't a lot of conversation, and as soon as the movie was over, he drove me home.

I got the impression Mike didn't like me. I didn't even get a kiss at the door. I called Susie the next morning to ask her if she heard anything.

"Oh, he likes you well enough," she said, "but your dad and his friends scared him."

I mentioned to Susie the three were harmless, and Susie said the shotguns they were holding were not. In shock and horror, I found Mom in the kitchen and told her what happened the night before. She was sincerely annoyed with Dad; she told me to wait there, and she'd talk to him. I could hear her yelling at him from the kitchen.

Dad said they had gone hunting that morning.

"Did you have to point the gun?" Mom asked.

"The guns were empty, and we didn't point them," was the reply.

As the discussion continued, I could hear less and less of the conversation. After a while, they were whispering to each other. Mom came back in the kitchen, trying not to smile. She said Dad was sorry, and if I gave him Mike's number, he'd call and make amends. I didn't give him the number, but I did go out with Mike again the following Friday. Looking back on the situation, Dad was right again: If a boy is going to like you, it doesn't matter what you look like or how strange your family is. He will like you.

We dated on and off again until Christmas. He bought me a friendship ring and gave to me on Christmas Eve. Mom noticed the ring as soon as I came through the door. She followed me upstairs and was all excited by it. We talked about it for an hour. I went downstairs and wiggled my finger all around while talking with Dad, but he didn't notice the ring. I finally asked him what he thought of the ring.

He pulled his reading glasses down on his nose and said, "It looks nice, but if I find out that you've been kissing him, I'll make you marry him."

I don't know why, but I ran away crying. Mom had been standing at the doorway; as I climbed the steps, I could hear her voice get stern with him. A couple minutes later, he was in my room. With my head buried in the pillow, I could hear him walk closer to me. He put his hand on my shoulder and didn't move it.

He asked me, "What should I say to my only daughter who is growing up? I guess my old joke didn't go over well." I wanted to stay angry with him, so I kept my head in the pillow. "It's a very nice ring, and I think you and Mike make a cute couple. If you would like, invite him for Christmas dinner."

I made the mistake at looking at him. He smiled and melted my heart, and the anger I was holding left me in a hurry. Mom confided in me later that he knew I had gotten the ring. He heard us in the hallway "cackling" about it.

Mike and I dated the rest of the school year. In May, Susie and I were eating lunch with some friends. We were talking about prom and getting out of school.

Susie mentioned, "You've never been called to the principal's office."

"Never been caught," I quipped back.

Then on cue, over the loudspeaker, we heard, "Katherine Brown to the principal's office."

"See there, it happened!" I shouted.

Everyone was cheering as I left for the principal's office in a victory dance.

I arrived at the office to see the principal holding my dad's shoulder and shaking his hand. Dad turned to me, and the look on his face sent shivers down my back. He came over and hugged me without saying a word. My first thought was Grandpa had died. He hadn't been doing well since Grandma passed away the year before. Dad took me by the hand and led me out to the car. Mom was in the passenger seat and had a stunned look on her face. Dad tried to speak and then started the car. I could hear him sniffling and choking all the way home.

We were pulling in the drive when Mom spoke up. She said they just returned from the doctor's office, adding, "The doctor said the test I took on Monday came back positive for cancer. It appears to be in most of my body, and we must go to the oncologist this afternoon. You're a big part of this family and should be there with us."

At seventeen, a person is looking for adults to recognize them as grown-up, but right then, I wished they hadn't. Dad stopped the car short of the house; he opened my door, crawled in, and held me tight. I can't remember when he held me tighter. The next thing I knew, Mom was in the back seat with us. We sat there and cried for almost half an hour. Dad was the first composed. He got us all in the house and made some coffee, and we sat at the table and talked.

Dad said it was my decision to go with them to the oncologist or wait for their return. I asked what could be done, and Mom shook her head. Dad explained the doctor said it was very bleak.

"What does that mean?" I demanded.

Dad continued to explain the cancer had spread to many parts of the body, and chemotherapy would only delay the inevitable. The oncologist appointment was at three o'clock. The phone rang, and Dad instinctively picked it up. Through the tears in eyes, I heard him say, "Have Rob handle it."

The seriousness of the situation really hit home. I never heard Dad say that before; he'd always answer questions from work.

We all drove to the oncologist's office in Cleveland. The doctor showed up quickly. He explained that the test results from our doctor just arrived, and he needed some time to review them. About an hour and a half later, he returned. After reviewing the test, consulting with other doctors, and calling to verify the validity of the test, he concurred with our doctor that the outlook was bleak. He pulled out the MRI that Mom underwent on Monday. He showed us pictures of the liver, kidneys, and pancreas. They all had dark blotches that the doctor indicated were growths, and the biopsy showed them to be cancerous. Furthermore, the lymph nodes all showed cancerous growth. Her lungs were clear, but the doctor indicated this wouldn't last long. With chemotherapy, she'd have at least six months, maybe a year. He wanted to run his own test in the morning and would have a better answer for us. The three of us discussed the situation and agreed Mom should have further testing. She asked how long she'd have if she didn't get treatment. The doctor said four to six months. The doctor would have her admitted and have the test done early in the morning.

We stayed in the doctor's office until they were ready for Mom. She asked our opinion about forgoing chemo. She explained she had seen what chemo does to patients and really didn't want that life. Dad remained eerily quiet while Mom and I deliberated the subject.

I asked Dad for his thoughts, and he replied, "Let's wait until tomorrow."

We wanted to go up to the room with Mom, but the nurse asked if they could get her settled in her room first. Mom told Dad and I to go eat. I tried to talk with Dad all through dinner; finally, he told me not to talk with my mouth full. He usually enjoyed talking during meals. Meals were a time for enjoyment, sharing thoughts, and bonding. Tonight, it was something necessary to survive.

We arrived at Mom's room an hour before visiting hours ended. Dad gave me the keys to his car and told me to come back in the morning. I had ever driven his car before, but he gave me the keys without a thought. He would sleep in the lobby, but he wasn't leaving. The nurse said the hotel across the street would put us up and give a discount if we mentioned our situation. The test would last until nine o'clock, and we'd be able to visit after she returned.

Dad and I made our way over to the hotel. The manager said they had no rooms available. Dad told him that Mom was at the cancer ward across the street. The manager leafed through some papers, searched the computer, and found one room he could let us have.

The room had two full-size beds. I took the bed closer to the window, and Dad sat in the chair at the desk. After resting a couple minutes, he excused himself and left the room. He showed up a few minutes later with toothbrushes and a tube of toothpaste. I was in bed, fully clothed. Dad said he was going to get a drink. I asked if he'd like company; he smiled and waved for me to come. As he drank, we discussed the problems we encountered that day.

"What do you think of Mom not taking chemo?" he asked.

I divulged my innermost thoughts on the subject. When we finished talking, we agreed that we'd understand if Mom wanted to forgo chemotherapy. Dad thanked me for being there. I thanked him for treating me as an adult.

The next morning, I awoke to an empty room. I was in the bathroom when the door opened. Dad had a change of clothes for both of us.

"I guess we didn't plan this trip very well," he said.

He had gone out and bought a shirt, pants, and clean underwear for me. It all fit comfortably, even the bra. Mom was surprised that we were cleaned up when we were finally able to see her. Her surprise turned to astonishment when she found out Dad picked out my clothes. He modeled his designer clothes for her.

The mood in the hospital room had gotten cheerful when the doctor showed up, just before lunch. He said that his test only confirmed the test from back home. He asked about starting chemotherapy. Once again, Mom asked what the difference was between getting the chemotherapy and not having it. The doctor thought hard for a moment and then said with therapy, six months to a year, with less than 1 percent survival; without chemo, four to six months. Dad and I both looked at Mom. She had seen what chemo does to other people. If there were a chance of her surviving, she'd go through chemotherapy.

"I really don't want to finish my life going through the side effects of chemo," she said.

The doctor prescribed a pain reliever and sent a painkilling regimen to our doctor for the duration of Mom's struggle.

The doctor released Mom to go home by the end of

lunch. There was a restaurant in downtown Cleveland Mom liked, and she asked if we could go there and eat.

Dad asked her, How do you feel?"

Mom replied, "With my hands."

I had never been to this restaurant, but I go back every year on that date. We all spent a long weekend together. On Sunday night, Mom took one of her pain pills. She said it was overkill for what she was feeling.

On Monday, Dad drove me to school. He drove to Grandpa's and brought him to see Mom, and then he picked me up from school. He was going into work and let them know what was happening and explain he wouldn't be in again until after Mom was gone. I got a huge lump in my throat with the finality of his statement. When I got home, there was a couch in the hall, just outside the guest room. I peeked inside, and there was a hospital bed with monitors and a medicine cabinet. I talked to Mom while Dad was out. She said it was important to her that I finish high school and graduate. My graduation would probably be the last time she left the house (our doctor agreed to come visit her from then on). She also wanted me to go to the prom with Mike.

I hadn't talked to Mike since last Wednesday. I called him up, and he said he had been waiting for me to call. He didn't want to intrude on us; Susie had told him about Mom's situation. Mom suggested I invite him over for supper that night. Dad got home, and as usual, he brought enough food for a feast. Having Mike over helped us finish all the food. I asked about prom night, and Dad said Mom had been planning my prom night for over eighteen years. I pointed out I was only seventeen, and Dad just smiled at me.

The week went uneventfully. Mike and I went to prom. Dad was right; Mom had been planning it for that long. She had everything planned to every detail. Mike picked me up, and Dad got mad at him for showing up in a "junkie car like that." Mike stood there with his mouth open, not knowing what to say. Just then, a stretch limo pulled up, and Mom and Dad started laughing. Mike didn't know what to do at first but eventually started laughing with us. Many classmates were heading for Cedar Point for the weekend. I wasn't going, and Mike stayed with me.

Mom announced on Monday that she wanted to go to the office and say goodbye to everyone. Dad would allow it only if she followed his rules. She'd have to stay in Rob's office and wait for everyone to come to her. She'd have to leave when Dad said so. Mom told him she may be sick, but she still gave the orders around the house. Dad didn't take her joke well, and his normally warm eyes turned icy blue; she agreed to his conditions.

Monday was Mom's trip to the office, and Wednesday night, she attended my graduation. As it turned out, it was the last time she left the house. I noticed she was popping aspirin on a regular basis. Dad suggested she start taking her medicine. She said she didn't like the way it made her feel.

Dad said it would benefit her to get used to the feeling, adding, "It's not as if you're going to get hooked on it."

Mom had Dad split the pills in half for her to get used to them.

Ol' Uncle Joe came over a couple times a week. He'd try to get Dad out of the house. I told Dad to go out, and I'd stay with Mom. She told him she'd enjoy the alone time with me. After Dad left, I went in to sit with her as promised. I thought she'd go to sleep, but she had a lot on her mind. Mom never did sleep while Dad was out of the house. It was as if she stayed awake so she could scare off death.

She told me about marrying Dad, way back when. She said he was a big show-off when he was young. It was the company Christmas party in 1966, and on the way to the party, they were discussing marriage in general. After they arrived at the party, Dad and Mr. Denkins started drinking, while Mrs. Denkins and Mom sat and watched them make idiots of themselves.

Mom explained, "When he got good and liquored up, he got up on the stage, grabbed the microphone, and asked me to marry him. We'd only been dating six months, and the drunken fool was asking me to marry him. The next morning, he must have been scared about what transpired the night before because he called me at seven o'clock. 'Did I ask you to marry me last night?' he asked. Yes was my answer. 'You did say yes last night,' he said. 'I never said yes last night,' I coyly replied. 'Why should I say yes to an inebriated proposition?' Your father said, 'I'm not drunk now,' and asked me to marry him again, and this time, I did say yes. We talked about an hour.

"I went downstairs after the phone call. Your grandmother had a wedding dress catalog out and already had the hall rented at the country club. I asked where she got the catalog. She'd ordered it a month ago, saying, 'I can't wait for you two to make up your minds.' I asked how she knew, and she replied, 'Jack looks at you the way your father looks at me.' By the time the morning was over, we had the wedding planned."

I had never heard this story before. As I listened intently, I wondered if it was the drugs or just the need to speak with me before she died. She told me during one of our many talks to be patient with my husband. Men, she said, can be dense and not notice signals as they should.

I always thought Dad to be a complete man who saw everything; I asked, "Even Dad?"

She told me, "Your dad was especially difficult to train. He thought he knew everything. At twenty-four years old when we married, he was set in his ways. I had to train him in everything from picking up his dirty clothes to satisfying me sexually. Mr. Macho thought when he was done, I was done. I let him get away with it one time, but the second time, I took control and showed how to satisfy me."

This whole talk on their sex life was more than a little creepy.

Mom continued, "After that, each time, I'd lead him to the right spots. I'd direct his hands or slow him down as needed. Now he's an accomplished lover. I'll tell you another key to a happy marriage: never let him leave home without kissing you goodbye. A couple days after our honeymoon, he was going into the office early and didn't want to wake me. I think he made more noise trying to be quiet. Anyhow, I was awake when he left. I didn't call him at work that day. When he got home, there was no supper ready for him. He asked, 'What's the matter?' I looked him in the eyes and calmly said, 'If you ever leave this house without kissing me goodbye, you can just stay at work.' I knew then the only mistress I had to worry about was work. It's important you don't nag; it's easier to nudge him in the right direction. But sometimes, nagging is the only way to get a man to move."

As time went by, the drugs made her less coherent. She started repeating herself and forgetting where she was in a story. Her stories were very emotional, and in her sickened and intoxicated state, she cried a lot. Dad was getting thin. A couple times a week, Ol' Uncle Joe would show up and get Dad out of the house. I know they had drinks together, and Dad would sleep for a while afterward. I pointed out to Mrs. Ledbetter how thin Dad was getting. From that point forward, almost every day, someone was getting Dad out of the house and making him eat. I'd confirm what he ate each time. Dad was taking care of Mom, and I was taking care of Dad.

On the morning of September 4, 1991, Mom said the pain was gone. Dad had been administering medicine by pushing a button on a machine. He gave her the last dose at eight o'clock. At lunchtime, Gail came to take Dad out to eat. Mom had already asked Dad not to go, and he didn't. As the day progressed, Mom seemed to get very clear in her thoughts. It was the most coherent I had seen her in over month. Her not getting her medicine troubled me. When Dad went to the bathroom, I asked if she wanted some. She said it was all right and she was in God's hands. She was smiling and almost seemed delirious. Dad sat and talked to her all day. I watched them for a while. It was as if they were twenty-five again, and their love was brand new. Dad had his hand gently touching her. As Dad, with his rough hands, stroked slowly back and forth, Mom was gleaming with life.

Ol' Uncle Joe showed up and looked in on Mom. This

was the first time Dad didn't leave Ol' Uncle Joe alone with her. When the visit was over, Ol' Uncle Joe was amazed by her revival. I told him she hadn't had any medicine since early morning and didn't seem to need it. Ol' Uncle Joe called the doctor and told him the time was near. The doctor showed up and met with Ol' Uncle Joe. They didn't want me to hear what they were saying and were whispering in the den.

I went in to see if Dad required anything. He was leaning very close to Mom, listening intently to her voice. He kissed her and said, "I love you." There was a broad smile on her face. As he pulled back from the kiss, Mom's face went blank. Dad called me over and held me. I looked at the monitoring equipment; the lines were flat, and all the numbers were registering zeros. I felt sad and happy at the same time. It was very confusing for me. I wondered how I could feel happy when my mother just died.

Dad turned to me with a smile on his face and said, "Now, she's in better hands than mine." He always knew what to say in demanding times. It wasn't so much what he said but how he said it that made the difference.

Ol' Uncle Joe handled all the arrangements for Mom's burial. He either took us out or had us over his house for Aunt Maria's good Italian cooking. There was a private wake for the family at his house, and Grandpa attended. The next night was a public viewing for everyone to attend. The church held about three hundred people. I don't think there was an empty seat in the church.

Ol' Uncle Joe described the first time he changed Mom's diaper. He told me, "No one had smellier baby poop than your mother." I couldn't help but laugh at the anecdotes told about Mom. I tried to think of something amusing to tell everyone, but all I could think of were the talks we had while she was dying.

The day after we buried Mom, Dad was reading the Bible when I got up. I asked if he was all right. He said yes and asked how I slept. I asked what he was reading, and he said the Bible and suggested that I read it too. For the next few months, most of Dad's reading was from the Bible. He always was good at relating to the Bible, but his knowledge grew with every day. Dad was a good cook, but some nights, we dined at a restaurant.

At Thanksgiving, we had about a dozen invitations for dinner. Dad thought it was best if we ate with Grandpa; we were the only family he had left, he said. Dad and I argued who should cook this meal, and we agreed to cook it together. I made the stuffing, since I had watched Mom make it in the past. Dad usually only watched football on those Thursdays, but that day, he made everything else. We had a wonderful time at Grandpa's house. On the way home, Dad suggested I go see Mike.

"Thanksgiving is for family," I said.

Dad gave me one of his looks. He insisted I go out with friends that night. This was the first time I heard him say, "I love you," to me, and I wasn't sure how to take it. Him saying "I love you" weighted heavily on me all night. For my entire life, he always said, "Luv ya."

I had been driving Mom's SUV from the time she was no longer able to use it. At Christmastime, Dad took me to the dealership and traded Mom's car in on a new car for me.

He said, "Now that Mom is gone, you need good transportation to and from school."

He bought me a smaller, sportier car with good gas mileage. It should have been wonderful, yet in some way, it disappointed me. He seemed to be pushing me away. Grandpa never bought Mom a car, I remembered.

I went to Ohio University, starting the winter semester. I'd call him every night at first to see how he was doing. Every phone call ended with that vexing "I love you." The next summer, Dad asked me what I thought of him going to college.

"Not Ohio U," I joked.

"No, the local college," he replied.

I thought it would be great for him. I always knew he was smart enough for college. We discussed him going to college for about a week before he decided to go through with it. He had Gail Ledbetter help him make the arrangements. At first, I thought it was nice of her to do this, but then I thought he was just pushing me out of the way again.

I did go with him to buy school supplies. I joked with him about him buying me school supplies years ago. I asked him if he remembered taking me clothes shopping. We had an enjoyable time that night. I went off to school three weeks before he did. I offered to come home, take him to school, and get him situated. He told me to study hard, and he'd be able to find his way at school. I had heard of colleges requiring every freshman stay on campus for their first year but thought they would make an exception for my forty-eight-year-old dad. Dad got himself a deluxe room on campus in a coed dorm. I told him to be careful of those loose coed girls. He chuckled and rolled his eyes at me.

It was the last weekend in October before I could get home. It was Saturday afternoon; Dad and a nineteen-year-old girl from school were in the kitchen. Their books were on the table, and they were studying. I made a comment about him bringing girls over to the house unsupervised. He seemed embarrassed by this. I found out a little later they had no classes together; they were roommates.

After she went home, Dad and I went out for dinner. He asked me if I heard from Mike. I explained Mike and I broke up directly after I started at Ohio U. He asked if I was seeing anyone. I got the impression he wanted to focus on my private life because he didn't want to talk about his. I had plans to meet Susie and left him to pick up the tab from dinner.

The next morning, I tried to talk Dad into going to church with me. He said it was uncomfortable for him to go to church at this time. After church, we had lunch together, and I wanted to bring up the subject of going to church with him, but his demeanor scared me off the subject. I left for school, never bringing the subject of church to his attention.

The next few years slid by quickly. At the beginning of my senior year, I met a boy named Brian Williams, who would become my husband. Mom was right: When you meet the right person, you know it right away. I brought him home for Christmas break. He spent a couple days with us before going to see his family. Dad made him stay in the fourth bedroom, and you had to pass over some squeaky floorboards to get out of it. After Brian left to see his family, I asked Dad about him. He seemed neither hot nor cold about him. He didn't say anything bad about Brian, but his demeanor was a little cold.

I pushed on the issue, and he said, "He's a good boy." I felt this was his way of pushing me away again. I was looking for his approval but received a wishy-washy response from him.

When Brian and I got back together in January, he told me his mother was had given him the third degree about me. His father told him to come clean with his mother, and she'd go easier on him. I told him I wasn't sure if Dad liked him or not.

Brian asked, "How so?"

I explained the response I got when asking Dad about Brian. Brian joked that at least he didn't point a gun at him. We laughed it off. A little later, I asked him what he thought about getting married, since his mother was pressing the issue. Brian avoided answering the question better than a seasoned politician.

On February 1, 1996, Brian and I went out to dinner. He seemed nervous as we went to the restaurant, which neither of us could afford. All through dinner, he fidgeted and barely ate his food. I knew something was up when he told the waiter to bring dessert. A couple of minutes later, the waiter brought over a platter with a domed lid on it. He set the platter in front of me and pulled off the dome. There in the middle of the platter was a diamond ring. I stared at it for a moment and then saw Brian down on one knee, and he asked me to marry him. Looking back, it was not very original, but it was romantic and very unforgettable.

I called Dad when we got back to my dorm room; I said Brian had kissed me, and we had to get married.

"Who is this Brian?" he asked.

After I sighed, he congratulated me. I couldn't tell if this news excited him or not. Brian called his mother, and I could hear her screaming from across the room. Brian was the only boy of four children; he said he was a momma's boy. His dad got on the phone and congratulated him. This was one time I really missed Mom. Men don't get as excited about weddings like women do. They get excited about seeing their children married, but not the wedding itself.

I needed two more classes to graduate and decided to take them in the summer so we could be married in September. During spring break, Dad said he'd pay for everything if we got married in my hometown. This was agreeable to everyone. One morning, Dad took me out for a drive. I didn't know we were going; he kept it a secret until we got there. It was the premier bridal shop in the Cleveland area. He sat there with me while I tried on every dress. I could tell by his glassy eyes he was tired, but he stayed on to the end. I came out wearing a dress I liked a lot and was looking for a sign to buy it or not.

Dad looked at me and said, "I wish your mother were alive because this is too hard on a man."

Most of the dress designs emphasized the breast; I picked a dress that was not so revealing. Dad broke out his credit card and bought it.

Gail Ledbetter offered her help with the wedding plans. By July, I had reached the breaking point with Dad. He seemed out of his realm, and I called Gail for help. She was a godsend. I told her that Dad wasn't being helpful. He was offering solutions to problems I had solved, and when I asked him for his opinion, he'd reply, "That's your decision," or "Anything you want."

Gail told me men were dense about some things, like weddings. To men, a wedding was something you did to get married; for women, it was so much more.

"Don't blame your dad," she said. "My John was the same way when our daughter got married."

At the rehearsal dinner for my wedding, everyone broke up into small groups. Brian's mom had cornered me and was talking my ear off. I looked over and saw Brian and Dad talking intently. Suddenly, Brian broke out in laughter. The longer they talked, the more Brian was laughing. For two guys I thought didn't like each other, they were sure getting along.

The day of my wedding came, and Dad, who was normally composed, seemed terrified and ecstatic at the same time. He helped me get ready as best he could. Gail was the one who helped me into my dress. After eight fittings, my dress fit like a glove and was hard to put on. Dad saw me in my wedding dress for the first time and mentioned how beautiful I looked.

"It better," I snapped, "for what it took to get me into this dress."

He said, "You won't have that problem getting out of it."

I started laughing, and Dad added, "You look like your mother in that dress. I wish she were here to tell you things a mother should tell their daughters on their wedding day. I don't have the right equipment, but I will try to answer any of your questions."

I asked what he'd say if I were his son getting married.

Dad smiled and said, "Kiss your behind goodbye because it belongs to her." Then he ruined the moment by saying, "I love you."

Brian and I went on a weeklong honeymoon (that was all his new employer would give him). It took about a week to settle into our apartment, and I took a position with a nearby company. I invited Dad over for dinner on the following Sunday. Dad and Brian were watching football and talking. There seemed to be a lot of talking; when I was growing up, talking during a game would get you thrown out of the room, possibly even the house. I moved closer to hear what they were saying. Dad was telling Brian the sooner he got used to me being in charge, the better he would be. Dad was a leader in industry, yet at home, he was just another stringed puppet for Mom to boss around.

Brian said it sounded like being whupped.

"And proud of it," Dad quipped.

There was a pause in the discussion, and then Dad asked if I was listening in on the conversation.

I joked, "No, I'm spying on you two."

I asked Dad to come over every Sunday for dinner, but he said, "A young couple needs to have their space." He did manage dinner with us about once a month.

Brian took up golf for work, as he told me. Every Saturday morning, he'd gather his clubs and head out to the course. It only cost twenty dollars for golf, and he spent another five on beer afterward. This went on for six weeks or so; one Saturday, he came and mentioned something Dad had said to him.

"When did you talk with Dad?" I asked.

It turned out Brian had been playing golf at the country club with Dad every Saturday. I told Brian it really didn't bother me that they were friends.

Dad showed up for dinner the next day. I asked him how golfing with Brian was. Without missing a beat, he said great. While I was cooking, they were in the living room, talking very quietly. I peeked around the corner at them, and both went mute. I figured there was only one thing they could be talking about, and that was me. Right after I returned to the kitchen, they started laughing. This time, I marched into the living room and confronted them.

Brian said Dad was telling him that when a girl grows up, she turns into her mother. It didn't bother me that Brian agreed to this. He never met Mom.

Coming from Dad, was something entirely different.

Dad added, "See, just like her mother, when she's trying to think of something to say, she crinkles up her nose."

Brian pointed at me and snickered. This sent a white-hot flash through me, and all I could do was stare at Brian.

Dad said, "Boy, I'm glad I'm not in your shoes right now."

I turned my attention to Dad, and he went silent. The two of them didn't have much to say the rest of the evening. I found out later, Dad had told him about "the look" and said he could get me to do it.

Brian said, "Your Dad was right; the look is a scary sight."

It took us a little over two years of being married to save up enough money to buy a house. We were looking at houses and stopped by a big ranch on three acres. It had big bedrooms, with one painted to look like a nursery.

I told Brian, "This will come in handy," and he said

he wasn't ready for that. I told him he had less than nine months to get ready.

He started to tell me he wanted Dad to look at this house when it dawned on him what I had said. He was so happy, he told the Realtor we would take the house and then turned and asked if I liked it.

Brian's job took him out of town every now and then, and Dad agreed to be my substitute birthing coach, if needed. The three of us went to Lamaze class together; Dad almost passed out when they showed a film about childbirth.

He said, "With your mother, I was at the bar drinking cheap beer, and they called me when you were born. I don't think this is natural."

I replied, "They call it natural childbirth."

Brian was in town the day I went into labor. Dad waited down at the bar for him to call. Brian's family drove up from Cincinnati while I was in labor. As it turns out, both new grandpas were in the bar when their granddaughter was born. The new grandpas took Brian out to eat and brought him home to clean up. He took a week off to help me out with Caroline. Brian's parents showed up the next weekend, and Dad brought dinner over. The three men were downstairs most of Saturday night, talking. Since I had been pregnant, Brian's mother and I had been getting along better. She offered me advice as to what to expect from Caroline and Brian. Apparently, Caroline was going to be a bigger help than Brian. It was nice to have someone to talk to in troubled times.

She told me, "Nuts don't fall far from the tree, and Brian is a big nut that fell from a bigger nut tree."

The men came up from the basement with solemn looks on their faces. Dad went home, and Brian's parents went to bed. It was almost feeding time, and Brian changed Caroline's diaper. We were talking while the baby nursed. I told Brian his mother thought he turned out just like his dad. He seemed all right by this news. In fact, it seemed to make him a little happy.

I added, "It won't be long, and you'll be cleaning your ears with your car keys."

He gave me a look like "What's wrong with that?" He told me the two dads were giving him advice for helping around the house and said he'd try to accomplish as much as he could.

The next night, Brian volunteered to make supper after his parents left. He burned the meat, the vegetables were salty, and the mashed potatoes were soupy. We went out to eat that night. He came home early on Wednesday and offered to cook again. I told him to let me do it. He held the baby while I cooked. The baby went to sleep, and he watched television. I suddenly remembered Mom saying Dad couldn't boil water, and yet after she died, he cooked some fantastic meals for us.

The next Sunday, Dad showed up for dinner. I was telling him about a hypothetical husband who pretended to burn dinner to get out of having to help around the house and said this hypothetical husband had a very rough life after that. I added that I knew of two older men, who would remain nameless, who wouldn't tell a young father to do this.

"Hypothetically," Dad responded, "if a young man was doing that, I'd have to tell him it was wrong."

Brian was a lot more help after that hypothetical discussion. I did let him slide when, after changing a soiled diaper, he almost vomited.

Caroline was about six months old when the stolen wallet incident took place. Dad was due to have dinner with us on a Thursday since we were visiting Brian's parents on the weekend. He showed up late for dinner. Apparently, he had found a wallet on the street that day. He called the chief of police (they co-chaired the MDA telethon for the county), who said he'd have an officer meet him and pick up the wallet. Before the officer could show up, though, a plainclothes detective arrested him for stealing the wallet. It turns out somebody had been snatching wallets taking money and stealing the credit card numbers.

The detective handcuffed Dad and took him to the police station. The young assistant district attorney who had been spearheading the investigation found out that the police had arrested my dad and took charge of the case. He told Dad there were going to be no mistakes and he was going to charge him with the theft. Dad said they spent a couple hours making accusations without asking any questions. The police chief had been a meeting with the mayor and city council for the afternoon and stopped by the office before heading home. He saw Dad sitting in an interrogation room. Dad explained to him what happened and how he was treated. The detective and assistant prosecutor showed up and said they were ready to file charges. They checked 911, and there was no call of a lost wallet.

Dad told them he had only one witness to his

innocence. They asked who, and he pointed at the police chief. Since they never searched him, Dad reached into his pocket and pulled out his cell phone. The last call made on it was to the police chief to report the found wallet. The police chief pulled out his phone and showed them Dad did call and talk to him. The detective said he didn't see any cell phone. Dad pulled out the earpiece, which had fallen into his jacket when they arrested him. Dad asked if there was anything missing from the wallet, and they just looked at each other.

The police chief, detective, and the assistant DA went away for a while. When they came back, the detective told Dad he was free to go.

Dad said, "I don't think so. Someone owes me an apology."

The DA said that was not going to happen. Dad pointed out several violations in laws and regulations regarding police conduct.

Then he turned to the police chief and said, "You know me."

The police chief and detective went into the chief's office. There was a heated discussion, and the detective returned and apologized to Dad. After that day, anytime Dad compared me to Mom, I always said at least she hadn't been arrested for stealing wallets.

One Sunday morning in June 1999, I was pleasantly surprised when Dad attended church. He came with Mary Osterhauf, a nurse who was divorced ten years before and attended our church. The next few months, Dad was his usual self at church. Brian and I were at his parents' house the first weekend in September. We got back, and Dad seemed to have changed. He was just as confident and fun, and had that powerful manner about him, but something was different. The biggest change was, he was thanking God for everything. When someone sneezed and he said, "God bless you," it had more meaning in his voice.

At Christmastime, this new and improved Dad hadn't changed back, and I asked him about it. He said for the first time in his life, he knew God. He realized Jesus died on the cross for him, not for everyone, but him.

I asked him to explain, and he said, "When I knew that Jesus died on the cross for everyone, it seemed like a pleasant thing to do. It was an impersonal and distant thought. Now, I know Jesus died for me; it makes all the difference in the world. Jesus didn't die for everyone; he died for each one of us. Then I realized he didn't die *for* me; he died because of me, because I'm a sinful creature, and the only way for me to be saved was him dying on the cross. For over fifty years, I've struggled to understand this simple message. I read the Bible and other books, trying to understand this message. Then one day, I considered my own heart and realized the answer wasn't in some book but in my own heart. There was God, waiting for me. It was as if he said to me, 'Where have you been?' A big lump of pride and self-righteousness came up, spilling a vile taste into my mouth. God choose me to be a follower."

The next Sunday, I looked at God in a brand-new light. I first thought it was Dad's light, but it turned out to be a brighter light than his. I knew what Dad meant when he said he could hear Jesus talking to him. I heard the same voice telling me everything was under control. I realized by me trying to do everything, nothing seemed to be done. I started asking for God's help every day and soon was asking for help in everything I did. Christmas, starting that year, meant so much more than it did in the past.

One Saturday morning in February 2000, Brian and I had been up late and were hoping for a little extra sleep. I could hear Caroline singing in her room. I nudged Brian, but he covered his head with a pillow. A mom's job is never done, so I got up to see my baby and her cuteness in the morning. When I opened the door, my usual amazement turned to horror when I saw my little girl with her diaper off, playing with the fresh deposit of poop. I hollered for Brian, and he came running as if the house were on fire. We used baby wipes to clean her up, and I immediately washed her bed coverings.

I called Dad in hopes of getting sympathy. Instead, it gave him a good laugh when I told him what happened to his granddaughter. He told me it was entirely Mom's fault. This left me puzzled, and he explained that when I was about Caroline's age, they woke to a similar incident, only I had poop in my hair, up and down my back, and in my mouth. I got it all over the crib, the sheets, and the wall. Dad carried me crying into the tub and cleaned me while Mom scrubbed the nursery.

After everything was cleaned up and we were eating breakfast, Mom told me, "I hope you have a little girl who poops all over herself, the bed, and the walls." Therefore, I could blame Mom for my daughter's antics.

The next year flowed by quickly, and at Christmas of 2001, I found out I was pregnant again. Dad was hoping the trend of girls would stop and we would have at least some testosterone in the house. On Groundhog Day, the sonogram showed the stem on the apple, as Dad put it. Life couldn't have been better.

But on April 10, 2002, I found out it could get a lot worse. It was two o'clock in the afternoon. It was a very lovely day for April in Ohio. The sun was shining, and it was about seventy-five degrees. When the phone rang, I thought it was Dad; I had just been thinking about him. It had been a couple of days since we last talked. I was going to run some names by him for his grandson.

The hospital was calling; Dad was there, unconscious. They needed me to come and fill out some papers, since I was listed as his next of kin. Susie agreed to watch Caroline, and Brian met me at the hospital. I couldn't visit with Dad, but I could look at him through the window in the intensive care unit. He was hooked up to machines, and tubes were going and coming from every part of his body.

Finally, the doctor showed up and explained the Dad had a massive heart attack. The doctor rambled on about valves and electric current to the heart and massive damage inflicted.

"Is he going to live?" I shrieked.

The doctor explained the machines were keeping him alive. He would need a heart transplant to have a chance.

I called Mary Osterhauf, who had been dating Dad for the last couple of years. I told the doctor to tell Mary what had happened so she could explain it to me. They talked for what seemed like an eternity, and Mary came and explained everything the doctor said. She said it didn't look good for Dad; she didn't think he'd make it through the night. The next morning, Dad went into cardiac arrest, and after working on him for an hour, the doctors pronounced him dead.

The next few days were dreadful. Brian showed me why he had been the right man to marry. He handled all the arrangements, including caring for Caroline. His parents came up and helped that week. There was a private memorial and a public gathering. There were speeches by mayors, township trustees, and business associates who knew him at the public viewing. Rob Owens got up and tried to speak. A large church in town held the public viewing; for most of the night, there was standing room only.

At the private viewing, Terrell Denkins got up and told the story of how they met. His father had been a drunk, and his mother worked all the time to put food on the table. He got into some trouble and quit school at age fifteen. He bummed around for many years, until one day, he went to a party at a park in our county. He woke up Monday morning with no money and no way back home. Mr. Sterling gave him a job. Jack taught him how to run the machines. Terrell explained he had been born one day before my dad was, yet my father was a better influence on him than his father had been. Jack also taught him how to read and helped him earn his GED. Jack showed him how to save money and straightened out his head when he and his wife were having problems.

Brian got up and told about Dad's role in us getting married. He said Dad pretended not to like him because he knew if a girl found out that her daddy liked the boy she was dating, she'd drop him like a rock. Dad told him Grandpa didn't think they were right for each other, and that was what made Mom interested in Dad.

He said that at the rehearsal dinner, Dad offered him one piece of advice for marriage: "Kiss your behind goodbye because tomorrow, it will belong to Katherine." This was the first time I had heard this story.

Speaker after speaker came up and talked about Dad. I knew he was special, but the number of people whose lives he touched was amazing. It was cold and rainy the day they laid Dad in the ground. Brian wanted me to stay home because of the baby within, but there was no stopping me. I had to agree to conditions before he'd allow me to go. I stayed in the car until everything and everyone was in place. The pastor said a prayer, and they lowered the casket into the ground. I said my last goodbyes and said, "Luv ya," to him one more time. Mary said she was meeting some of Dad's friends at a restaurant in town that evening after the public memorial. It was not too far from the funeral parlor, and Brian agreed to watch Caroline if I wanted to go.

These friends of Dad were all female. I recognized one girl, who was less than a year older than me. She was his roommate at college. She told the story of how Dad changed her life. Another girl worked for Intricate Stamping Company; she was Dad's girlfriend. She too had a story of how he touched her life. Some of the women got a little graphic in their relationships with Dad. Mom had been right when she said Dad was an accomplished lover. A young reporter for the county newspaper stopped and asked everyone questions about Dad. He was still with them after I left. Mary called me a couple months later and asked if I was interested in contributing to a book on Dad. She asked me for some stories, and I told her Mrs. Ledbetter would probably want to help.

Dad had set up a college fund for Caroline and our unborn child. The attorney who was executor of the will told Brian and me that the memories we'd build together were worth more than any money he could leave us. Dad set up several charities to receive the bulk of his estate. The last thing in Dad's will went to Mr. Colachi. The attorney called Ol' Joe "sir" several times in a brief period. As Ol' Uncle Joe was about to say something, the attorney explained that the will had instructed him to do that. Ol' Uncle Joe just sat there and shivered. I wasn't sure, but it looked like tears in his eyes.

As I got closer to my due date, I asked Brian about names for our baby boy. Brian said it was the first mention of this subject since Dad died. I told him about the phone call from the hospital and explained that I had hoped to talk with Dad about some names. Brian thought long and hard and said he'd like to name our son Jack Brown Williams. I told him that sounded wonderful.

He said, "The boy will have some large shoes to fill with this name."

Between losing Dad and Mom, losing Dad was much more devastating. When Mom passed away, we all knew the end was coming. I had a chance to say goodbye. On her last day, she was awake and alert. I told her how much I'd miss her and gave her my love. There was a sense of relief as she passed on to God's hands and her pain left her body. There was an additional comfort, knowing Dad was still with me.

Before Dad passed away, he was unconscious the last eighteen hours. I was not able to get close to him in the ICU cardiac ward. He left me without saying goodbye and without me telling him how much he meant to me. Since Mom died, he had been telling me, "I love you," and I always wanted to ask him what happened to "Luv ya." I had so much to tell him but never got around to it. He was so much of who I am today. Dad always knew what to say to either infuriate me or make me feel better. Most of all, I'll miss those chameleon blue eyes. They could be so warm and melt the coldest of hearts, but at times, they were so cold they would scare off the devil himself. I'll miss you, Dad.

Chapter 3
by Bonnie Palmer Harrison
(Jack's First Girlfriend)

It was the first week in September of 1992, and I was starting my sophomore year of college. I got the same room as I did the previous year, which meant I didn't have to move anything. I lived in the coed dormitory, which was an experiment on campus. The university combined three rooms with four separate sleeping quarters. The walls were soundproofed, and there was a small central communal area for all to share. The bathrooms were down the hall.

I arrived early Sunday morning; Gloria, my new roommate, moved in on Saturday. Steve, another roommate, brought his gear up around two o'clock, and a half-hour later, his father showed up with a small television for the public area. Steve was disappointed because cable access had to be paid for in advance. We used the cable as an antenna. We received an Akron PBS channel and a couple of Cleveland channels. We all wondered who had the fourth bedroom.

Around six o'clock, this old man came in, carrying a small overnight bag. I was waiting for his kid to show up with the rest of the stuff. The old man went into the bedroom and came back out a few minutes later. He introduced himself as Jack Brown and shook everyone's hand. It was like shaking hands with a wrench (after Jack went to bed, Steve said he thought the gorilla was going to break his hand). Jack pointed at the TV and asked if we were stuck with it. Steve said the thirteen-inch model was his. Jack said he could do better, if Steve didn't mind.

Steve said, "Go for it."

I got the impression that Steve was planning to be the dominant male. He was the macho type, and the world had to revolve around him. Before Jack arrived, Steve took over every conversation we had. Jack, however, was interested in Gloria's opinion and mine. We talked about our classes and our expectations for the future. Steve disappeared halfway through night. At ten o'clock, Jack said it was time for bed. Gloria and I stayed up to midnight, talking. We both commented on what a great man Jack was.

Gloria said, "If he were a few years younger, I'd marry him."

On Monday, Jack showed up about five o'clock; a local store delivered his new television during the day and set it up. When Jack turned on the TV, he got about a hundred channels of static. I told him no one had the money for cable and we were using the cable line as a normal antenna. Jack stated he would buy the cable, but we would have to come up with the money for any special channels. Steve said it would take him two weeks to cable hooked up, and he'd have to pay in advance to get it. Jack pulled a phone out of his jacket pocket, pushed a couple buttons, and said hello, followed by "Don't you owe me a favor?" He explained the situation and said he wanted to be able to watch the stock market show at six o'clock.

About a half-hour later, there was a knock on the door; it was the cable worker, who said he needed to check the connection. He pulled the cable off the back of the TV and hooked it to a meter, then he called down to someone and said he was getting a good signal. He reconnected the television and turned it on, set the channels, and made sure everything was working properly. Jack came out and asked how it was going, and the cable worker said they were finished. Jack grabbed the remote and changed the channel for his stock show. He signed the cable worker's paperwork and thanked him. Jack asked if they were working all night, and the worker explained the boss requested them to work overtime for this job. Jack brought two twenties out of his pocket and told him and his unseen partner to have a beer on him. The worker shook Jack's hand before leaving. Jack sat down and watched his show.

After his show, Gloria came home, and the three us of got involved in conversation. Steve showed up and went into his room with a sour look on his face.

The school had a rule requiring freshman to stay in the dormitory. Jack had an early-morning class on Tuesdays and Thursdays, and he stayed in the dorm on the nights before. We were welcome to use the TV anytime, but if we watched MTV, he asked us to keep it down when he was there. The three of us ended up watching Monday Night Football until halftime, and Jack went to bed.

That Wednesday night, after watching his stock show, Jack went into his room and studied. Friday morning, Steve was moving his television out of the dorm. When

I got back from class, his door was open, and I peeked in. His room was clean and empty. We never saw Steve again.

The next Monday, the three of us watched football again until halftime. Wednesdays were my study night because Gloria had a pottery class and went out with friends afterward. I liked to lounge in my underwear when studying. After a while, I threw on a robe and went out to see Jack. I watched the last of the stock market show with him. This was the first time he and I were alone together. We talked in depth about me and in life in general. I could not help but notice how hot his blue eyes were.

We had been talking about forty-five minutes when Jack stopped me in midsentence and asked me to put "that" away, as he looked down at my breast. Apparently, the last time I shifted in my seat, it popped completely out of its hiding spot. Embarrassed, he said he knew it didn't matter with young people, but he came from the old school and found bare breasts a distraction in conversations. I quickly put it back under cover. This changed the tone of our conversation. Jack tried to cover up his embarrassment by making a suggestive joke. I found his awkward ruse somewhat amusing and decided to challenge him. To my surprise, he met the challenge, and I found myself amid some heavy petting with him.

Looking back on the situation, I could see that Jack was trying to get out of the exploit his libido had gotten him into by saying someone may interrupt us. I explained that Steve had quit school and Gloria was out until after ten.

He then said, "We should stop; I don't have protection."

I took Jack by the hand and led him into my bedroom. Before leaving for school, my mom had bought me a box of condoms (she didn't want any grandkids before I graduated college). I always heard narrow-minded parents say if you bought your kids condoms, they would have sex. In this case, if they hadn't been available to us, we probably would've stopped.

Jack was very gifted lover. After we finished, he got up, gathered his clothes, and went into his room. I didn't hear from him the rest of the night. The next Monday night, Jack didn't show until nine o'clock. The only way I knew he came in was seeing his door close. I never pictured Jack as a love-them-and-leave-them type, but he was avoiding me.

The following Wednesday, Jack was on the couch when I looked out at six thirty. He turned off the television when I opened my door. I paused for a moment, and he asked me to come out. I sat next to him, as I did a week ago. In my mind, I was calling him all kinds of dreadful things. I looked at his eyes, and instead of hot, they were deep, murky pools of sad blue.

He started by apologizing for his behavior for the past week. He explained it was not like him to behave that way. He acknowledged I was a wonderful lover, and he appreciated the sacrifice I made for him.

"This is not an excuse for my behavior," he said, "but I'd like to explain my actions."

Usually, when a man tells you this, something lame is coming up next.

He said his behavior had to do with his wife. I was shocked to hear that.

He explained, "I was married for almost twenty-five years when my wife past away a year ago. In twenty-five years, I was never with any other women. I hadn't had sex since about six months before she passed away. I let my physical needs outweigh my emotional needs. After we finished making love, it felt as if I had cheated on her. Counting you and my wife, I have been with two women in my life. I thought it was an appropriate time to start anew, but the reality is, I still love my wife and am finding it hard to move on to other relationships." Again, he pointed out it was no excuse to behave badly toward me the past week, but I understood his anguish.

When he finished with his discourse, all I could do was hug him. We spent the next few hours talking about his wife. I found it interesting that he always referred to her in the present tense. He told me how they met. Sarah was the boss's daughter and pretended not to like him. She told him that he was arrogant and bull-headed, yet she showed up at a bar where he and other employees hung out after work. He said years later that he overheard Sarah and her girlfriend talking about that night at the bar. The girlfriend pointed out that Sarah insisted on stopping when she saw Jack's car outside the bar. She pretended not to be interested in him and ignored him every time he looked over. When Jack was not looking at her, though, she was looking at him. A friend convinced him to go over and talk with her.

"She dangled the bait in front of me and got me hook, line, and sinker," he said, smiling.

I had heard my girlfriends talking about finding their soul mates. If this was what they were talking about, then I'd like it too. Jack's eyes glistened as he described his wife. I wondered if one woman could be that great. I guessed she was, to him. Through his first year, we had sex on only two occasions. He always got a little depressed afterward.

Jack was an earnest student. Every time we compared grades, his were As, and mine were anywhere between A and C. During the winter quarter, I had a class that was causing major problems. I could not understand the material, no matter how hard I tried. Jack said if I started quitting now, I could look forward to a lifetime of quitting. He worked with me and helped me get through the class. He hadn't taken this class, yet he was able to make me understand the material. He always seemed to know what to ask to find the answer. He explained when faced with a problem, it was better to ask questions than try to solve it. This learning technique was an immense help in school and in life. I often rely on Jack's questioning approach with my kids.

In mid-February, our dorm had a party in the commons. The students hired a DJ to play music. Everyone was sitting around, listening and talking the whole night. I remembered thinking it was a pitiful party. The DJ went on break and set the player to some Loony Tune music. Jack got up on stage and started dancing and singing to the music, using a funny voice. Everyone was laughing at the sight. Another student got up on stage with him and started doing the same. Before long, there were several people singing to the music. Jack came back and sat down with me.

"I like your funny voice," I said, laughing with him (I found out later this was his normal singing voice).

He then grabbed me, and we started a conga line. The DJ was playing some old-fashioned music, but everyone was having a wonderful time. Jack went home at eleven o'clock, and the party continued. Several people asked if Jack could come back in a couple weeks.

One day, Bob, my old boyfriend, called me. Jack showed up while I was on the phone. I told Jack that Bob wanted me back. Jack presented me with some accepted wisdom: Bob had dropped me for a new girl, and now she had dropped him. He came back to the comfort he had before. It was easier for him to try for me than to go looking for something new. Bob dropped me once, and he would drop me again. Jack also pointed out that I had admitted I was more in love with the idea of having a boyfriend than in the boyfriend.

Jack added that I was not the same girl who left to go to school two years ago. I was older and wiser, and my taste in men had changed.

I said, "Someone more like you."

Jack insisted it could never be him; I needed someone closer to my age. Jack was happy with our friendship the way it was. I needed a man who came home hungry every night. It was all part of growing old together. When a couple is first married, he explained, they cannot keep their hands off each other.

He remembered, "When Sarah and I moved into our house, she spent the day cleaning, and she cleaned everything. She had old sweats on and a bandana in her hair when I got home from work. Her face was smudged from the work she had accomplished. She bent over to put something away, and I wanted her, right there and then. I grabbed her and started kissing and caressing her. She tried to fight my advances because of how she looked, but her love for me prevailed, and we ended up in the shower together.

"Another time," he recalled, "it was a busy week at work, and I came home exhausted. I sat in my favorite leather chair for a night of vegetation. Sarah brought me a beer. She started rubbing my neck as I drank the beer. Then she started to rub my chest. I groaned, 'I just wanted to sit here,' and she said okay. She stepped out in front of me and proceeded to strip. I don't mean she took her clothes off; I mean she stripped like a pro at a girly show. She really vamped herself for me. I didn't have to move; she did it all. Let's just say, I hadn't been that relaxed in a long time. I think she really liked being in control. Sarah took advantage of my love. When we finished, she said now we were even for me making her do it the day she cleaned house all day. We ended up eating cold cut sandwiches because her dinner in the oven was severely burnt by the time we were hungry enough to eat it. Those are the memories two young people can create."

I wondered what it was like when people grew old together.

Jack acknowledged, "We are not that old. Well, not old enough to where I need to ask her if I like beans or not. There is a comfort level reached after a while. Sarah hates the fact I was comfortable with her. I tried to save the situation by pointing out what I meant; it was comforting to know she would always be there for me. I don't think she bought it, but she did let me slide on it."

I interjected by asking about sexual activity at his age.

"Oh, that is comfortable as well," he said, laughing. "To tell you the truth, it gets better with age. It may not be as often, but what you get is fantastic. Each partner knows what buttons to push, and we had slowed enough to enjoy the moment. Moreover, with a child in the house, we had to learn how to schedule the event so we looked forward to the moment when we could be with each other. You come to the party prepared."

"So a lot of late-night rendezvous?" I asked.

"One of our favorite times was on Saturday morning. There was cartoon Katherine liked, and we could depend on her staying glued to the TV. Last Christmas, Katherine and I were talking about the old TV shows, and she mentioned that show and how she liked it. I told her, 'Mother and I liked it too,' but she said I had never seen it. I just smiled at her. Then she said neither Mom nor I ever watched the show. It took a couple of seconds, and she got what I was implying.

"When Katherine was in high school, there was always a dance, a game, or a club meeting in the evenings. We would always have those nights marked in red marker so we wouldn't forget to pick her up. Sarah and I really looked forward to those red marker nights and made the most of them. Spur-of-the-moment sex is nice, but planned out and expected is better."

I asked about monotony.

"First, when you're in love, it is anything but monotonous. In addition, you can always bring different things to the party to keep it new. There are different rooms in the house and various positions. Sarah bought a book one day that showed a hundred various positions. We tried some of them, laughed at others, and didn't think the rest were physically possible. To me, this is what made the relationship comfortable, being able to discuss freely any matter with my wife. I don't think there was anything

I couldn't tell her about myself. Half the time, she knew what was bothering me before I did."

If I was willing to settle for less, then I should not complain when my expectations were not met; that was his message. He had been reading the Bible when the conversation began.

He held it up and said, "This book can help you meet your expectations."

Ever since we met, he was reading the Bible, or a book about the Bible, in his spare time. It seemed to give him peace, yet he was searching for something in all those books. He wanted more than he had now. I was expecting a long speech about going to church, but he left it at that. I was gathering all the reason for not going to church, and he didn't say anything more. If I ever wanted to talk about it, it would be with him, I figured.

We were getting our schedules set for the spring quarter, and I asked Jack his advice on classes. I was a graphic design student and needed to choose some electives. Jack suggested I take some business classes and, if possible, make business my minor. He pointed out many engineers were laid off for younger engineers, and no one wanted to hire them at the money they were worth.

"The engineers who have management experience," he explained, "don't face this dilemma. As you progress in your profession, you will need to take on a management role in the company that employs you. It is best to prepare for such a day. Moreover, if you start your own company, which many in the art world do, you better have a good business sense, or you might lose your shirt."

I hadn't heard this from any of my college advisors.

Nearing the end of the spring quarter, tensions were high at college. Personalities that clashed all year sometimes erupted into violence. This was the case late one Wednesday night. Jack and I had been talking, and it was approaching ten o'clock. I knew Jack would be going to bed soon. It started as a quiet rumble in the hall. Two fellows were arguing. It grew in intensity with every word spoken. It didn't take long, and we could make out the words exchanged. Jack tried to ignore it, but then there was a bang against the wall.

Jack's eyes grew wide, and he leaped toward the door, hollering, "Hey!"

The two fighters, who were wresting on the floor, froze in their places. Jack had this serious voice and told them to stop it. I peeked out the door, and both just stood back.

"What's going on?" Jack asked coldly.

The two of them just looked at each other and shrugged their shoulders. I was worried about Jack getting involved with a couple of hotheads. They both just backed down from this old man. His voice had much command; they stopped what they were doing.

The dorm monitor opened his door after the ruckus stopped and asked what happened. I thought it was funny he didn't show up until after everything quieted down. Campus police arrived a minute or so later. Jack talked to the police and persuaded them to ignore what had happened. The dorm monitor wanted to press charges. Jack finally turned toward him and stared him down. Without saying a word, Jack got the monitor, who had been talking brashly, to say it was okay. He turned to the boys, told them not to do it again, and went back into our room.

Over the summer, I got a part-time job working at an ad agency as a graphic designer. They were willing to work around my studies and made it a permanent position. I got a room off campus that allowed me more quiet time. Jack didn't renew his dorm after his first year. We would meet once a week, usually on a Tuesday for lunch. We kept each other informed as to the problems and delights in our life.

During one the luncheons, I told Jack about Kevin Harrison, a boy I met. There was something about him, and it drove me crazy. Jack smiled and asked if he was worth keeping. I shook my head and said maybe; I said I wanted him to meet Kevin.

"Is it a good idea to have your new boyfriend meet your old boyfriend?" he asked.

I replied, "You were not really a boyfriend."

"We slept together," Jack answered.

He didn't need to know; that was my explanation.

Jack looked at me as if he wanted to slap me and said, "Starting off a relationship on a lie makes for a rocky relationship. If you build a house on a soft foundation, the first storm will wash it away. If you build your house on a foundation of rock, then no rain or wind will break it."

I recalled him telling me that he and Sarah had not had sex until their wedding day, which made their honeymoon special.

Jack told me to tell Kevin he was worth waiting for but Jack was not. He continued by saying, "If a man is going to love you, then he will love you. You must present yourself totally to him. If he rejects you, then it was never meant to be; if he accepts you, there won't be any surprises for him later. To me, Sarah was the sexiest women I ever met. Even near the end, when her back pockets got filled out and her boobs were sagging, there was no other woman who could touch her in my mind."

It was loving sentiment, but I didn't think Sarah would approve of his description of her.

Two and a half years later, I graduated, with a business minor. The day after graduation, Kevin and I were visiting with his parents. His mom asked me when I was going to make an honest man of her son. What was it with moms and their sons? His dad told her to leave us alone and apologized for his wife. Later that day, we were heading to see my parents. Kevin brought up what his mother had said. We had discussed marriage as an institution in the past, but now, he seemed to be feeling me out for a response. I told him if he wanted to know if I'd marry him, he'd have to ask me. To my surprise, he pulled the car off the road. I figured at that point, he was either going to throw me out or ask me to marry him. It was the latter. In my excitement, I forgot the actual words he had said.

We got to my parents' house and told them. My stepdad congratulated us, and Mom wanted to start planning everything out that night. Dad asked what Kevin's parents thought of the idea, and we explained it just happened on the way over here. He picked up the phone and told Kevin to call his mom and tell her. Kevin made the call, and his dad answered.

Kevin told his dad, "Tell Mom we became engaged on the way over tonight," and he hung up the phone.

I stared at Kevin, and he said, "What? If I talk to her, I'll be on the phone forever."

Just then, the phone rang. It was his mother. My dad got up and left the room so Kevin could talk with her. I don't think she was pleased to find out about our engagement the way she did.

I sat next to Kevin while his mother spoke to him. I could not hear what she was saying, but she sounded excited. Kevin finally got a word in and then said, "Here's Bonnie," handing me the phone.

My mom got on the other phone, and we talked about the upcoming nuptials. When we finished, Dad and Kevin were in the kitchen, sucking on suds, as Dad would say. Mom offered to put clean sheets on my bed for Kevin and me. I told her Kevin would be sleeping in my brother's old room. Mom said we were out of college and getting married, and she wouldn't mind having grandkids now.

Kevin and I both had good jobs in the Akron area. It was a forty-five-minute drive to either of our parents' house, and we figured it would be a good place to settle down. Kevin wanted to move farther from his mother, because she would come over often if we lived too close. I didn't know what his problem was with his mother; she and I get along well. The house we picked out was about twenty minutes from Jack's house and was a local call.

Soon after we were married, Kevin got up one Sunday morning and invited me to go with him to church. I declined. I called Jack while Kevin was at church. He asked why I didn't attend church. I explained my mom forced me to go to church every Sunday, and I hated it. Jack asked if it was the church or being forcing to go that I hated. After some intense thinking, I realized it was the forcing. Jack explained that church was not so bad; it can be quite a lot of fun. If you didn't like preaching, there were plenty of other activities to enjoy.

I asked Jack why Kevin suddenly decided to start going to church.

He said, "First, you should ask Kevin, but when a man marries a woman, the two become one in sprit. It changes the man. Without woman, man cannot be complete. Without God, marriage is subject to more problems than it can handle. The responsibility a man takes on when marrying a woman is much greater than when he was single, and it is only natural for a man to find help with the added responsibility. Then again, he may be thinking that is what you do when you get married; men are creatures of habit."

I asked why he didn't go to church, and he snapped back, "I'm not married."

The following Sunday, I started going to church with Kevin. Jack was right; church was not that bad when you volunteered to go.

Kevin discovered he liked having barbecues. We started small, with just the neighbors coming over. After a while, it became a Saturday-night ritual, with many people attending. Jack would call once a month and ask, "What's for BBQ?" and Kevin would invite him over. We got our first snow in late October that year and figured the BBQs were over for the year. To my surprise, you get better flavor when barbecuing in the cold; we barbecued year-round.

The next summer, Jack suggested a deck for our house. Jack and Kevin got all excited at the prospect and started planning our new deck. The next Saturday morning, he showed up at seven o'clock with a friend named Ol' Joe.

I had sketched out what I thought would be nice, but Ol' Joe abruptly stated, "That's no good."

We had two plans: one Jack and Kevin drew, and mine, which I modified from Jack and Kevin's sketch. Using stick figures, Ol' Joe drew out a third option, incorporating what I wanted with more functionality. Ol' Joe said we needed more space for chairs and the grill. His design used less wood, and we could access the basement to run a gas line out if we wanted.

By eight o'clock, the three headed for the lumberyard. They got back in an hour with a load of wood on the back of Ol' Joe's pickup truck. That day, they sank the posts in the ground and cut all the wood to size. Sunday afternoon, they finished the project. Kevin grilled some steaks for everyone, and we all sat out on the new deck. During the warmer months, it is the most used room in the house.

In the fall of 1999, Jack called me one day. He said the Lord had opened his eyes, and he could see. He explained what had happened to him. One memorable thing Jack said kept running through my head for the next couple of weeks: "Jesus didn't die for everyone; he died because of me." Years before, he had suggested I talk with my husband about matters of the church, which I ignored. Now I was afraid to ask Kevin, and I could not bring it up to Jack again. The past few weeks had been very eventful. No one thing had made it difficult, but everything together had put me in a stressful condition.

I had heard our church offered a day care while you were at church. I made an appointment with Pastor Bob to speak with him, and he arranged day care for Kevin III and baby Jill. I told the preacher about the problems I was having. To complicate things, I had been wondering more about God. I even tried to pray to him for help. A couple of weeks earlier, I prayed for patience while I figured all this out.

At hearing this, the preacher chuckled. He immediately apologized for that response and explained that God had answered my prayer.

"How so?" I asked.

"The Bible tells us you learn patience by trials and tribulations," he said.

We talked for almost an hour about God and the church.

Intellectually, it all made sense, but something was missing. I walked down the hallway to pick up my kids when I passed the sanctuary. It was dark except for one single light on the cross. The reflection gave the great hall a luminescence to it. I saw how beautiful the cross looked. I walked down the wide passage that led to the cross. I was about halfway there when Jack's words came back to me about Jesus dying because of me. *Because of me?* I kept repeating in my mind. "What did I do?" I asked defensively. Then I felt my heart turn cold, and every wrong I ever committed had a hold of it.

One by one, each of those wrongs revealed themselves. The guilt of not talking with my husband when I should have, minimizing my mom's role in my life, yelling needlessly at the kids, and more placed a heavy weight upon my heart. I wanted to cry as each was exposed. The guilt had been a part of my life so long, I didn't want it to leave. There was a voice in my head telling me it was not yet time to cry. I felt my knees get weak and sat on the floor, waiting for it to end. Just when my heart was so filled with these guilty feelings I thought it would explode, with a tiny click, they were all gone. There in my heart was a peace, a peace I had never known before, and it was time to cry.

I lay there, crying tears of joy. All the guilt from all I had done my whole life was gone. In its place was peace, love, and joy, which only God could put there. Suddenly, I understood. Everything I read in the Bible made sense. Jesus was real. He was alive, and he was God. He died, was buried, and rose so at this very moment, my sins would be forgiven. Pastor Bob showed up and asked if there was anything wrong. I smiled and said everything was all right. We sat on the floor and talked some more about Jesus.

It was April 11, 2002, and I hadn't heard from Jack in over a week. I remembered we had a very good BBQ the past Saturday. Kevin served Cornish game hens from a spit. I called Jack at his house to gloat over the delicious meal. Brian, Jack's son-in-law, answered the phone and asked who I was. I explained who I was and asked Jack to call me back.

He said sadly, "Jack cannot call you back. He passed away today."

At first, I thought it might be a joke; it had to be a joke. Jack was always so full of life. There was an awkward silence as I waited for the punch line, and then all I could say was "Wow." Brian said he knew how I felt.

The next day, I got a call from Brian, telling me there was a private viewing for family and close friends on April 15 and a public viewing on the following day, inviting me to both. There were about fifty people at the private viewing. I appreciated being at this function. There were people from all walks of life there. Everything seemed to revolve around his daughter, who I had met once back in 1992. Several people who had known Jack longer than I gave testimonials about him and what he meant to them. I noticed what they said about Jack corresponded with my feeling for him.

Jack was a strong and compassionate man who gave of himself entirely. I don't think he ever left anything half-done. I never met anyone who had a bad thing to say about him. There were people smarter than him, but I have yet to meet anyone wiser. He had a way of looking past the image you portrayed and seeing the real you and accepting you for who you were. He has joined his wife in God's hands.

Chapter 4
By Mary Beth Lassiter
(Jack's Second Girlfriend)

In May 1992, I divorced my husband of ten years. One day, I went to his office in downtown Cleveland, planning to surprise him, wearing nothing but a teddy under my coat. I was hoping to have lunch at a nearby hotel and spend a couple hours with him. His secretary was not at her desk when I showed up, which helped me with my surprise for him. I loosened my coat, flung open his office door, and howled in surprise. The surprise was on me because his secretary was on the couch, and my husband was on her. I don't think he wanted an afternoon delight after that.

I let out a blood-curdling scream and then had a few choice words for my husband and his secretary. I don't remember ever using those words before, and I hope there's never an occasion to use them again. I closed my coat and ran for the elevator. I passed my husband's boss running down the hall. There were several coworkers peeking out their office to see the commotion. The elevator doors were open when I arrived. I was tying my coat as my husband ran down the hall, still putting his clothes on. He was yelling to hold the elevator. As the doors closed on the elevator, he was still tucking in his shirt.

By the time I got home, my pain turned to anger. I was furious at him and wanted to hurt him back. As the afternoon progressed, my anger subsided. I thought about our family and the importance of keeping it together. We could work this out, I decided. It may take all night, but I was determined to make it work. I sent the kids, Jane and Michael, to my mom's house for the night. I cooked dinner for just the two of us and set up TV trays in the den. I figured it would be most favorable for a long talk with my husband.

I was expecting him to be apologetic and humble when he arrived; instead, I got a man who was yelling at me for causing a ruckus in the office. He was mad because I caused a scene and his boss saw it. He had to sweet-talk the boss just to keep his job. For a moment, a very small moment, I was ready to give in to his ranting with an apology of my own. He acted as if it was my fault he was doing his secretary on the couch. Then I remembered what caused my outburst. I took the dinner and threw it in the dog dish (it must have been from across the room because the next day, there was quite a mess to clean up). I put on my coat and left for my mother's house.

We went to court about six month later. He tried to deny having an affair with his secretary. His boss's wife and I were on the same PTA committee, and she told me what her husband and the other employees saw that day (the secretary was still topless when he looked into the office). They all agreed to testify for me in court.

The judge was not happy with my husband. I got the

house, and he got the payments until the kids were grown. The judge ordered him to pay $750 per child and $1,000 alimony per month and keep all three of us on his health care until Michael, the younger, was eighteen or finished with college, whichever was later.

On July 24, 1993, my alimony was reduced to $500 per month, since it was deemed a hardship on my ex-husband. I was going to have to find a part-time job to make ends meet. I needed a couple things at the grocery store and picked up a newspaper to see if there was anything out there for me. I was in a hurry to get home and start my search. The grocery store had just installed barrier that beeped when shoplifters tried to take things out of the store. I cut around it to save a step and made a hard turn around a concrete wall. Just as I got by the wall, I ran into someone. I'm barely five feet tall, and the only time I weighed more than a hundred pounds was when I was pregnant.

My head bounced off the man's chest, and I found myself sitting on the ground, looking up at his polished blue eyes. The look of surprise on his face just made his eyes glimmer. He immediately apologized for the collision and started picking up my few groceries. He helped me off the ground with his rock-hard hands and insisted on buying me a cup of coffee at the in-store restaurant.

I declined at first, but then he gazed at me with those brilliant blues eyes, and I agreed to a cup of coffee. He wanted to make sure I was all right, he said. He made a mistake by asking me what was wrong, because I spent the next half-hour telling him my life story. Most men would have gotten a glazed look on their face, but he seemed genuinely interested in my mess.

I told him about having my alimony cut in half and said I was looking for a part-time job.

He said, "Don't you mean a position?" He explained that a job was something you did, while a position had growth and meaning.

"I'd like a position," I replied, "but who would hire me for a position with two kids to worry about?"

He told me of a company about twenty minutes from Medina, which was near my home. He said the president of the company told him that very morning how it would be nice to find someone to do data entry on a part-time basis. The person needed to be proficient at the keyboard and be able to read the information going into the computer. That sounded very interesting to me, and I wanted to know more. He didn't have any more information but said I should contact the personnel manager at Intricate Stamping Company.

"Can I use your name?" I asked but then realized I didn't know his name; I asked what it was.

"I'm Jack Brown," he said, "but don't use my name. I don't know if the personnel manager likes me or not." He gave me his card and told me to let him know if I got the position.

Upon arriving home, I looked up the number for Intricate Stamping Company. I called and spoke to Karen Colvin in personnel. I asked if they were looking for someone, and Karen said she just got out of meeting where they discussed that subject. She told me it would be a part-time position for several hours during the day, and they would be willing to work around other scheduling problems such as day care or school. I made an appointment for the next day and met with Karen. She had me type a story into the computer. I noticed a couple of misspelled words and asked her if I should correct them or leave them as they appeared. After the interview, Karen had me wait while she went and checked on something. Upon her return, she told me I had the job and would start on Monday at eight dollars per hour.

When I got back home, I called Jack to tell him I got the position. He was very excited for me, and I offered to cook a meal for him and his wife (I had assumed he was married, since he was wearing a wedding band). He explained he was a widower, but he would be pleased to have dinner if the offer was still open. The kids were going to their father's that weekend, and I offered to cook for him on Friday night.

That Friday, I fixed a potpie for him. I've won awards at PTA cook-offs with this recipe. It's my best dish. My ex was late picking up the kids, and they left just before Jack arrived. I was frantic and getting flustered by everything happening at once. I didn't greet him at the door properly; I told him how sorry I was about his dead wife, but that was not how I wanted to say it.

Jack understood my situation. I've always had a problem with saying something meaningful and having it come out horribly. I calmed down as he talked with me. His voice was smooth and relaxing. I had talked about my life during our first meeting and asked him about his life. While I finished cooking, Jack told me how he had to support his family after his dad died; he married the boss's daughter, bought the business, and retired when she came down with cancer. I noticed that whenever he mentioned his wife, Sarah, he did so in the present tense, as if she were still alive. After dinner, I thanked Jack for the tip on getting the position at ISC.

We talked for a couple hours about my new job, the kids, his daughter at college, and many other things. There was something safe about Jack. Somehow, I knew he wouldn't hurt me or take advantage of me. Around nine o'clock, he suggested he should leave. I mentioned I hadn't been with a man since before the divorce. Jack just looked at me. I told him he didn't have to go and invited him to spend the night. He seemed very surprised by my suggestion, mentioned an early-morning appointment, and said he wanted to leave. I went over and kissed him straight on the lips. It must have changed his mind because he spent the night with me. He did get out early the next morning, and by lunchtime, flowers arrived with a thank-you note attached. I called his house and left a message saying I had nothing to do until Sunday night, if he would like some company.

He took me out to eat that night, and we ended back at my place. Sunday morning, we discussed the weekend, and I told him I preferred not bringing men over to the house when the kids were home, and I didn't like leaving them with babysitters.

He asked, "Is this goodbye?"

I said it was, until next month when their father picked them up.

I reported to work on Monday at nine o'clock and met with Karen. She gave me an introductory package with the company handbook, and we went over my schedule. The kids were in school from early morning until three o'clock, and I wanted to be home when they got there, I explained. This worked well with the company's plans. Karen said the job required about twenty hours a week to enter all the information.

She asked how I heard of the opening, since it hadn't been advertised.

I told her, "Jack, a man I met, told me to call, but I was not to mention his name, since he didn't know whether you liked him or not."

She asked, "Jack who?"

"Jack Brown," I replied.

She took me into the hall and pointed at a picture on the wall; it was Jack, before his sideburns turned gray.

"That's him," I said.

She called Jack and asked why he didn't want me to mention his name. Jack explained that he didn't want to influence her decision. This meant I got the job on my own. He told me later it was up to me to keep the job.

The week before the kids were to visit their father, I called Jack to see if he was free for the weekend. He had plans for Friday night, and Saturday, he was attending a barbecue. My heart sank because it didn't sound if we were going to meet up. He asked if I'd like to go with him to the BBQ. That sounded great, as I tried to hide my delight. Jack picked me up at one o'clock for the BBQ. I decided to wear a dress and high-heeled boots. Someone as important as Jack would have a fancy BBQ, I supposed. He showed up wearing tennis shoes, old blue jeans, and a short-sleeved shirt. I could tell by his eyes he wanted to say something, and I asked if I should change.

He replied, "At least those fancy boots."

We went to some friends of Jack's; it was a family get-together, with four generations attending.

Jack's friend, who owned the farm that surrounded ISC, said any friend of Jack's was a friend of his. Later in the day, the host told how they became friends: "It started back in 1942; the war was on, and everyone was making sacrifices. There was a push to get more food to market to help our troops. Mr. Sterling made a deal with my dad to farm the eighteen acres next to the company's building. In return, my dad would pay Mr. Sterling two dollars an acre at harvest time. After the war, my dad wanted to keep farming these fertile acres and offered Mr. Sterling more money to do so. Mr. Sterling told him not to bother, just plant some sweet corn for him, and we'd call it even. So every year, my dad would pay Mr. Sterling $36 and all the sweet corn he wanted. I bought the farm from my dad in 1969 and in 1970 bought the Connelly dairy farm. Jack bought ISC in 1972; even though money was tight for him, he kept the same arrangement, knowing the tough times farmers were having. In 1973, Sarah was having a baby and ISC was on the rocks; me and the missus sent a side of beef to Jack so they could at least eat. Since that time, when something needed to be rebuilt, Jack would let me use their machine shop."

I had a lot of fun at the barbecue and wished the kids could have joined me. I beat Jack twice at horseshoes.

Every month, we would meet for a weekend to relieve the tensions that built up. The following year, my ex-husband sued for custody, claiming I was having wild sex parties while the children were home. He named Jack as leader in these activities. All the parties at the house were having a bad influence on the children. He cited several parties and had dates to back up his claims.

My lawyer said the hearing was in two days, and he just got the list of offences claimed by my ex-husband. Jack suggested that my lawyer not respond to the claims until we got to court. A year earlier, Jack had talked me into keeping an organizer for dates and times. I found by writing appointments down in the organizer, I could remember them with no problem. The last six months, I had listed every meeting, party, and event in the organizer. The three of us looked at the list of complaints by my ex and compared them to the organizer. One of the parties my ex noted was a Tupperware party, which my daughter helped host. A couple of dates were PTA committee meetings, and the last was Jane's tenth birthday party for her and her girlfriends. The lawyer asked how many times Jack had met the kids. Counting today, Jack said, the total was zero. The lawyer asked Jack to be at the hearing, and he said he was already planning to attend.

At the hearing, my ex's lawyer said he hadn't gotten our reply and was not ready for court, which seemed to upset the judge. My lawyer pointed out we got the list of complaints just two days before the hearing. There had been no time to review the complaints, but he was willing to go through with the hearing. The judge told my ex they had over a month to send the information, and they would have to deal with not knowing our response. My ex got up on the stand and gave his list of complaints just how we received them. My lawyer took each of his complaints one by one and shot them down. He had my organizer, and each date my ex claimed I had a wild party, he pointed out the truth. My daughter's birthday party, which the ex failed to show, was last. The judge's jaw almost hit the floor when he found out it was my daughter's birthday party, and it was eight ten-year-old girls going wild.

"What about the wild sex she's having with some old man?" my ex blurted out.

Jack got on the stand and said we only got together when the kids were at the ex's house. My ex's lawyer asked if there were any other men in my life, and Jack said he didn't think so.

The lawyer said, "You can't be sure if you're there only once a month."

"No," he replied, "but a man can tell when a woman has not had sex in a month," and everyone but my ex laughed at the comment.

The judge asked if Jack had ever met my kids and then later confirmed with the kids, in a closed-door session, that he had not.

The judge was so mad at my ex, he ordered the child support to go up to $1,000 per child per month, and my ex had to pay all court costs, including my lawyer's fee.

"The next time you want to get out of paying child support," the judge yelled at my ex, "you better have your story straight." The judge added if he lost his job for any reason, he was still responsible for the child support, insurance, and house payment. The first payment he missed, the judge would see him in jail.

There was something in the way Jack answered the questions that day. No one challenged him. When Jack said something, it was believable and accepted as true. I can be overly trusting at times and thought it was just my reaction to Jack, but it seemed the rest of the world saw him the same way.

The subject we talked about most in our monthly meetings was his wife, Sarah. Jack didn't mention her during our third monthly sleepover. It was nice because we focused more on me that month. A couple days afterward, I realized that I had missed hearing him talk about Sarah. I marveled at the way he referred to her as if she were still alive. Sarah became a friend of mine through the stories he told. While talking with a friend, I mentioned Sarah as if I had spoken to her the week before. If she was half the woman Jack described, she was incredible.

One of my favorite stories Jack told me about Sarah was the birth of their daughter, Katherine. I had heard him say on several occasions that say he was in a bar, drinking cheap beer, when Katherine was born. I told him it was not a pleasant thing to say, and he explained, "We were eating breakfast at six o'clock in the morning, and Sarah was feeling sick. This was strange because she didn't get sick during the first few months, when most women did. I had just started eating breakfast when she ran for the bathroom. Something was out of the ordinary about it, and I followed her. She left the bathroom door open, and for Sarah, this was unique. She always closed and locked the door so I wouldn't know what she was doing in there. Yet if I followed her, there was no mistaking what she had done in the bathroom.

"She looked at me with those big brown eyes and said her water broke," he continued. "My first instinct was to check the commode for leaks. Then in a bolt of lightning, it hit me: The baby was coming. We had a bag packed in the closet for this time. I picked it up, but it was empty. The same bag her mother used, and now it was empty. She scolded me and said to grab the other bag. I turned to say something about being fickle; her face was beet red, and her eyes were bulging. It only lasted a minute, and I asked if she was having a contraction. She glared at me and sarcastically said, 'No, I was just trying to get my eyes to pop out of their socket.' I thought it best not to ask any more questions until this ordeal was complete.

"We were almost to the hospital," he went on, "when she had her second contraction, which was about twenty minutes later. She wanted to wait until the contractions were closer, but I insisted we leave right away. They took her up to a room. The doctor on call got some information. She told the doctor we should have waited to come in until she was about ten minutes apart. The doctor explained with the water breaking, it was better we came now. I started to gloat about being right when the third contraction started. This was very bad timing on my part. The sweet angel I married turned into a raging monster for about a minute, and I had to hear about it when the pains had passed.

"I spent almost every minute with her throughout the day," he said. "At noon, her contractions went from twenty minutes to thirty minutes. At four o'clock, she hadn't had a contraction for forty-five minutes. About every hour during the day, a nurse would come and build a tent around her legs and call out, "One." After a couple times, I suggested if they found two of them down there, they should call Guinness. I was in trouble again.

"Her OB/GYN was now there," he continued, "and

explained this could take a couple hours or all night. Sarah asked me if I had eaten anything all day. I mentioned breakfast and the Jell-O from the so-called lunch they brought her. She said I left more breakfast on the table than I ate, and Jell-O didn't count as food. She told me to go get something to eat. I didn't like hospital food, and she suggested the cute diner we passed on the way. So I went to the diner, which looked so good from the outside.

"It wasn't much more than a honky-tonk," he said. "This nice diner from the outside was a grungy bar on the inside. They had two kinds of beer: cheap and cheaper. When I say two kinds of beer, I don't mean just on tap, but in the whole place. Two kinds of beer, and they were cheap. Their menu consisted of a small chalkboard with hamburgers for fifty cents; the two other items they offered were swiped away. I ordered a cheap beer and the hamburger. The beer was cool at best. The burger took about a half-hour to get ready, and I order a second lukewarm beer. The burger was well-done, very well-done. In fact, it crunched when I bit into it. I thought at first it was crispy lettuce but remembered burgers don't come with lettuce. I could only eat a couple of bites from my crunch burger and choked down the warm, cheap beer.

"I couldn't have been gone for more than an hour," he went on. "As I walked down the hall to Sarah's room, everyone was congratulating me. I finally asked why, and a nurse explained I had a baby girl. Delight and happiness filled every pore in my body. It didn't take but two steps for me to realize I was at a bar when she was born and not by my wife's side. I never knew fear until that very moment." You could see the fear in his eyes as he told this part of the story. "I walked into the room and smiled, giving Sarah a big hug, and I hoped she didn't notice I had been missing in action. My father-in-law was happy to point out where I was at the time of the birth. 'Thanks a lot, Dad,' I grumbled. When the endorphins kick in during childbirth, it works wonders. This woman who was ready to hurt me before I left called me a wonderful husband who she forced to go out and eat something.

"Her OB/GYN said it was the strangest thing he had ever seen. He was on his way out for dinner when a nurse stopped him and said Sarah was at ten centimeters and crowning. Apparently, I wasn't gone five minutes when the contractions started again, and they were coming less than two minutes apart. A half-hour later, our baby girl was born. By the time I got back to the hospital, Sarah was back in her room, recovering. The doctor told me I had my hands full with this daughter of mine. She was already causing trouble. Sarah reiterated I wasn't in trouble, but she would bring up the cheap beer and crunch burger from time to time."

Jack was a good storyteller, especially when talking about Sarah. The faces he made while telling the stories were priceless. I got a foul taste in my mouth when he mentioned the crunch burger. Another story he liked to tell was when Katherine was caught drinking at age sixteen. With my kids approaching that age, it sounded like a good remedy for drinking.

I like country music, and in the summer of 1994, I took Jack to a nightclub that played country music. An old George Jones tune came on the jukebox called "He Stopped Loving Her Today." It's about a man who fell in love with an unfaithful woman. This sad man loved this woman until he died. Jack seemed welled up when he heard this song. The next time we met, I noticed a George Jones tape in his car. He explained there was something about the song he really liked. That night at the country bar, I tried to get Jack up and sing karaoke with me. I never knew him not to try something new, and with some coaxing, I got him to sing. He tried to tell me he could not sing, and he was right: He could not sing. For someone whose voice melted the coldest hearts, he sure could not sing. It was as if his voice was between two octaves and would go from one to the other throughout the song. If that was not bad enough, he had no beat. When the words came out of his mouth, they were all flat and without inflection.

We saw each other almost every month for a couple of years until I met Harvey, who was a divorced father of two, at a PTA meeting. Harvey asked me out, and his invitation sounded pleasing. Jack was nice, but Harvey piqued my interest, and nothing was coming out of my relationship with Jack. I gave Harvey my phone number and asked him to call me the next week. I told Jack about Harvey and the feeling I had when he asked me out. He said I should pursue this relationship.

"Be careful," he said, "and keep your heart and mind open because you both are carrying extras with you."

I asked if he'd still be able to give me advice.

"You got my number," he replied. At first, I thought he was referring to his phone number, but then I realized he meant much more.

My mother watched the kids when Harvey and I went out. We saw each other about once a week at first. My mother was a tremendous help in watching the kids. Jane knew I was dating and was all for it. She wanted to meet Harvey, and I brought him home to dinner one night. After we were dating about three months, Harvey said he was tired of hearing about Jack. I had to either stop talking about Jack or let them meet. The three of us had dinner together one weekend while the kids were at the ex's. Jack became a friend to both of us. I dated Harvey for two years. Until we got engaged, I never let him get close to the kids emotionally. We were engaged for a year before we set a date. I wanted to be sure our children adjusted to the idea of us being married. Harvey is a wonderful man, and Jane and Michael both loved the idea of me marrying him.

Harvey was a religious man who attended church every Sunday. I grew up in a house where we only attended church on Easter and Christmas. Harvey would talk with me about God, and I'd listen as best I could. From the years Jack and I saw each other, I remembered he always read the Bible or some other religious book. Jack and I met for lunch one day, while the kids were in school. We talked for almost two hours about God and religion.

Jack said many of the same things Harvey stated about living forever and the importance of being with God.

I asked Jack, "How do you know if you're going to live forever?"

He started sucking on his lower lip. I asked him about knowing God, hoping it was easier for him to answer. Both were very good questions.

He said he had read many books on the subject and talked with many people, and his only response was, "I guess you just know it."

I had never read the Bible, and Jack gave me a book on Calvinism. Calvin was a great thinker about God and church, and it helped me to understand. I wanted to know God for my wedding vows.

It was a week before the wedding, in the spring of 1999. I was home alone. Harvey was at work, the kids were in school, and Mom was off somewhere. I sat alone in a chair, a Bible and Jack's book on Calvinism setting beside me. I had been reading both and grew weary of the lack of answers. They both tell you how to live within God's laws, but neither explains how to know God. I started to talk with myself and eventually started talking with God.

I asked, "How do I get to know you? What do you want from me?"

My own voice inside my head said, "Just love me."

I thought about that short statement for some time: "Just love me." As I continued to talk to God, a warm feeling came over me. A tingling went down the side of my face, and my heart started pounding. I kept talking to God, and soon, I understood what it meant to love God and to have him love you.

I called Harvey to tell him the discovery I just made about God. I was telling him how warm and loved I felt at that moment. As I told him all I experienced during the afternoon, tears started streaming down my face. I told him how much I loved him and how I could not wait to get married to him.

Harvey said, "See, prayers do come true. I prayed you would get saved."

I was saved, and I was going to live with God through eternity. With this knowledge, a peace came over me, and

I knew from that point that everything was going to be all right. I knew difficult things would still happen to me, but it would be okay with God at my side.

I called Jack later that evening and told him about the experience I had. Jack asked me what I did to find God. I told him I just sat and talked to him. I told him how I was feeling and how I longed to know him. I always thought Jack knew God, but from his questions, it became apparent he didn't. Being new at this religious stuff, I didn't know what to say. To tell you the truth, I'm still not sure what I say to him; I just talk to him. I went back and started reading the gospel again. This time, it had much more meaning to it. Occasionally, Jack and I would talk about the Bible and God. If I read something and was not sure what it meant, Jack would tell me what he thought it meant. If I still had questions, he would refer me to other books to read. After one of my questions, I asked Jack if he found God, and Jack replied simply, "Not yet."

In the fall of 1999, I got a call from Jack; he sounded excited, as if he just hit the lottery.

"What is it?" I asked.

Jack rambled, "I found God; well, God wasn't lost, but I was. I guess God found me, but then again, he knew where I was. Anyway, I have accepted Jesus Christ as my savior. I have been speaking to God for the last year. My problem was, I hadn't been listening. You told me to talk with God, but you never mentioned to shut up and listen to what he was saying."

We both started laughing. I asked him about the peace you feel when the Holy Spirit takes hold of you. He answered with an awful rendition of "Amazing Grace."

On April 11, 2002, I returned from a two-day trip to a university in southern Ohio where Jane was hoping to attend. Harvey met us at the door, and his face had sad news written all over it. He looked at Jane and said it was about Jack.

Without thinking, I said, "Go ahead and tell us."

He told me he heard a rumor this morning that Jack passed away. I remember hearing my purse hit the floor and everything pouring out of it, but it didn't matter.

I stuttered, "Is it t-t-t-true?"

Harvey confirmed the worst. He just got through at Jack's house, and his son-in-law was there, answering phone calls. Brian stopped in at five o'clock to check on the house and answered phone calls all night. He confirmed the rumor. I thought back to when I accepted God and how peaceful it was and how everything would be okay after that. I accepted the situation, dealt with the loss, but still felt the pain of losing a good friend. Harvey grabbed me and held me tight. Jane and Michael had both met Jack and gotten to know him as a friend of the family. As a family, we sat and talked about death and God, how the two intertwined.

Brian called the next day. He informed us there was a private viewing for close friends and relatives, and I was more than welcome to come. Thursday night was a public viewing, which Harvey wanted to attend. Jane and Michael both said it would be nice if the whole family attended. After the eulogy was over, Mary Osterhauf approached me. She told me some friends of Jack's were meeting at the diner next door. Harvey took the kids home, and I joined the other women for dessert.

Jack was a good friend. If Sarah didn't preoccupy his heart, I probably would have married him. On the other hand, I never would have met the wonderful man I did marry. God does have his plan for us. It is comforting to know Jack will be with his beloved Sarah again in God's house. Everyone who knew Jack will miss him. He helped me through some tough times. I knew from that Friday night when I asked him to stay with me, I could trust Jack to do right by me.

Chapter 5
By Ms. Eddie Tobar
(Jack's Third Girlfriend)

It was the first Monday in April of 1996. I was the assistant to the director of a not-for-profit company raising money for breast cancer. The company was formed a year earlier by a consortium of local businesspeople. Our first year, we managed to forward just $125 to the charity. The previous Friday, the head of the consortium dismissed the company's director. She had a degree in charitable management and had previously worked for United Way. The chairman of the board of the company introduced John "Jack" Brown that morning as the new director.

The first week, Jack didn't say much and stayed in his office. The following Monday, he called everyone into his office and let two people go: Cameron Diesel, the marketing coordinator, and Clare DuPont, the project coordinator. Cameron, who graduated from Yale, worked part-time and ran his own marketing company. Clare had a sociology degree from Kent State. She worked part-time for the charity and managed a household full-time.

Without consideration for either of their situations, Jack told them they were free to go.

Jack appointed Kandi Balicki as the new project coordinator. Kandi was a secretary with three children and a high school education. She hadn't seen her husband in several years. I would handle marketing, with help from Jack. The charity went from a director and five employees to a director and three employees. Jack went on to explain that everyone was replaceable, but if we worked together, there would be no replacements.

He met with all the employees, one by one. I was the first to meet with him. He asked if I had any questions, and after what I saw that morning, I had plenty. Jack explained that the two college graduates didn't like to work. He spent the first week observing who did what and how much they accomplished. They were two peas in a pod who thought they were better than everyone else. He saw no results of any work they had performed during the first week. My results were enough to keep me for the time being, but I'd have to show better results soon. It didn't matter how hard you worked if there was nothing to show for it. He told me about a friend of his named Ol' Joe. When Ol' Joe was in the army, they had him move a pile of dirt in the morning, and in the afternoon, he moved it back. He worked very hard that day but had nothing to show for it. We discussed my jobs at the charity; I was very surprised at the depth and detail with which he described my jobs. He gave me until the next Monday to have at least four marketing ideas for raising money.

He sent for Kandi and had me stay and take notes. He told Kandi her performance was excellent but her duties were changing. He described Kandi's new responsibilities and gave her one week to compile a list of the projects the charity ran the first year. Jack wanted her to tell him how and why the projects failed. Jack assured her that either he or I would help her if she asked.

After she left the office, I asked Jack, "Why her?"

He had two good reasons: First, she needed the money with three mouths to feed. Secondly and more important, last week when she finished her work, she went looking for more.

The next day, Jack received a call from a corporate sponsor. He was the owner of the local business and a friend of Clare, who was no longer working for the charity. He called to pull his donations from the charity. I only heard Jack's side of the conversation. He said calmly that he would miss their money. He acted as if it was no big deal to lose this account. After a long silence, he apologized and reiterated that we would miss them, especially with our upcoming events and new marketing plans for corporate sponsors. He listened quietly for another moment.

"Well," he disclosed, "we are planning to put our biggest corporate sponsors on all our letterhead and list them on our front window for public recognition, and you're correct: The dollar a year I make is probably more than I need."

Jack became relaxed after this point in the discussion. By the time the two finished talking, he had a lunch appointment with this corporate sponsor. Jack handled the situation with flair and confidence. I found out from the secretary this sponsor had been extremely mad when he called. Not only was Jack able to keep him as a sponsor, he got him to double his donation.

On Wednesday, I asked Jack about my ideas. I didn't think they were any good. Jack asked how they compared to my previous ideas. No one ever asked me for my ideas before. Jack wanted to know how I knew they were no good. If his expectations were four promising ideas, he could have hired a top agency in New York.

Come Monday, I thought three of my ideas showed promise, and the fourth was something I scribbled down the night before. Jack, Kandi, and I sat together and discussed our assignments. It turned out we kept only one of my promising ideas, and the scribblings from the night before proved to be our first project. It was simple but effective, and it is still one of our best moneymakers. With the help of a local grocer, we sponsored a bake-off, featuring local favorites. All participants made two entrees, one for the judges and one for us to sell. The judging for the entrees were taste, appearance, and local tradition. The first year, we got twenty-five entrees, and this past year, we had over a hundred entrees. The first year, we made $290 from the entrees and another $500 in donations, with zero cost to us. This past year, with corporate sponsors, donations, and sale of entrees, we cleared $10,000.

As spring turned into summer, we became very busy in the office. We had scheduled four major events for the year, with plans to continue them if they worked. As the amount of work increased, so did the productivity of the office. We accomplished more with three people than last year with five. As we complete our contrasting functions, we grew in confidence and were having more fun. Jack was right: It doesn't matter how hard you work if nothing is accomplished. By the end of the summer, we had raised more money than we did the entire first year.

The first couple of months, Jack and I only had a professional relationship. That was more my fault than his. I was a little bitter about him taking over the charity. As the business grew, my respect and admiration for him grew. Throughout the summer, our relationship became more personal. It started by me asking about his wife. I heard him discuss her with others and assumed she was alive. You could imagine my embarrassment to find out she passed away five years before. He liked to talk about Sarah, and you could get him off any subject by mentioning her name. For the most part, our nonwork-related discussions were safe topics during the summer.

That fall, Jack started having me join him for business lunches and dinners. At first, I thought it was his way of making up for a lack of pay. He met with contributors at most of these luncheons and talked business. He always seemed to get his message through to the people, because we'd get a check a few days later. As I became familiar with the nuances of courting clients, I could see how Jack got from saying hello to having them agree to give money. More often than not, they would walk away thinking it was their idea to give money.

We had a client cancel for lunch one day, and Jack said we still must eat. We started by talking business. Jack said I was fishing for compliments, and it was not becoming.

"Don't ever show your fear," he said. "About a year ago, I was having dinner with a friend, and he told me about this company. He said they were not doing well and were losing as much as they brought in. I spoke up and said, 'How hard can it be?' Before long, I agreed to become the next director. I had no idea of how to run a company like this one. I had no practical experience in dealing with the public. My company only sold to other manufacturing companies, and now I was dealing with the public. I came into a new office in April and had to lay people off. Believe me, there is a lot to fear with all the newness. If I let the butterflies in my stomach dictate my job, we wouldn't be doing any better than the past administration." He was saying, show confidence in all that you do.

We were getting along well at lunch until we discussed politics. It was my belief the government should protect and help those who were in need. Jack believed a minimalist government served people better. I believed President Johnson's safety net, established in the 1960s, was the best thing to happen to America. Jack said nets only trap things, and President Johnson's Great Society trapped many Americans in the welfare system. It was like the animals that lined up for feeding every morning behind the office. There was free food, so why should they forage for it? As the discussion heated up, I noticed he sat cool and collected. For every argument I inserted, he would calmly rebut and challenge my stance.

We arrived back at the office after lunch. I was starting the afternoon work when I realized the extent of the discussion we had. I remembered how I got a little angry in my debating. In past employments, arguing with the boss usually meant not seeing the boss anymore. Your position became stagnant. Jack peeked into my office and said he enjoyed the lively discussion today and we should do it again some time. I was relieved to hear him say this. About once a week, we would get together and discuss political topics. I never could rile him, and through it, I learned to stay calm in discussing matters.

The first week in March of 1997, Jack scheduled a meeting with the chairman of the board and me. In the two years of working there, I had seen the chairman twice: the first day, when he introduced the director, and a year ago, when Jack was hired. If tradition continued, we were getting a new director. We met a local restaurant. Jack introduced me and explained that March 31 was going to be his last day. I was going to take over if I could pass this interview. He promptly left.

The chairman asked me if I wanted the position. I said sure, and he told me I was the new director.

"Was that the interview?" I asked.

The chairman said Jack highly recommended me to take over, and that was all I needed to get the job. He told me how much more I'd be making, and Jack agreed to stay on as an advisor.

When I arrived at the office after lunch, Jack was waiting for me. We went over my new responsibilities, and he asked who should move up into my position. I suggested Kandi, and he asked why. Kandi had worked closely with me and understood my duties, and on occasion, she did my job. I think Jack already knew the answer; he just wanted to hear what I'd say. He invited me out for a congratulatory dinner. I suggested I should take him out, since I was the new director, and Jack said that on April 1, I could take him out.

The nicest restaurant in town was a block down the road from us, and Jack took me there. We arrived at six o'clock, and there were several people ahead of us.

The host immediately greeted us, calling Jack by name and showing us to our table. From my seat, I could see a "gentleman" complaining to the host. This man kept pointing at Jack and me. He started for our table. As he approached, I could hear him cussing about us taking his table. He claimed they had been waiting a half-hour. I had seen his group of four enter the restaurant as we left our office, maybe a five-minute walk. The man's face was getting red as he cussed at Jack.

After about a minute of this man cussing at us, Jack turned his head, looked at the man, and said in a very cold voice, "Leave it alone."

This angry man took one step back; his scarlet face quickly became pallid. He walked away, grumbling under his breath. Jack looked back at me, and shivers went up my spine. Those normally warm blue eyes had turned arctic and hostile. He did an exaggerated blink and returned to the conversation, as if nothing was wrong. In that brief flash, Jack's eyes were cold and barren, yet full of a lifetime of rage and anger. There was a storm of certainty, finality, and mortality in those blue eyes. I never saw his eyes so cold, before or after this incident.

I told him his eyes had been so cold when he dealt with the irate man.

He explained, "It was a trick I learned to stay out of fights."

After I became director of the charity, Jack and I saw more of each other on a social basis. At first, I'd put the dinner on my expense report because we did talk business. Then one day, I realized we hadn't talked any business the night before and chose not to add the dinner on my account. Jack and I were as different as apples and oranges, yet there was something about him. I knew how a mosquito felt when hitting the electric zapper. He was charming, intelligent, and handsome. There was something very distinguished about him and irresistible.

After a couple of months of social engagements, I wanted to kiss him good night. I got home one night and was furious with myself for not kissing him. Then I got furious with him for not wanting to kiss me. I kept telling myself, "We're business associates, and a person with a degree in psychology should not feel this way." I felt like a schoolgirl wanting a boy to like me. The next time we went out, I had more than my usual glass of wine. As we were leaving, I grabbed Jack's hand, spun him around, and kissed him good night. Then I ran to my car and sat there like a frightened girl, not knowing what to do next. I started crying because of my childish behavior. I knew better than to act that way, but it didn't change the heart.

Jack tapped on the glass and smiled at me. Something in his big blue eyes convinced me to open the window. I tried to hide the tears from him, but they kept streaming down my face. I told myself to stop crying and sit up straight. I pushed the button to let down the window as I tried to compose myself. Jack asked if I'd like to talk or leave it alone. My first thought was to call him a dummy for not taking me and kissing me back. Then remembered I ran away, giving a mix signal. I unlocked the door so he could get in the car.

Jack entered my compact car and said it was impolite to kiss a man and run off. Maybe it was my nerves, or I knew he didn't hate me, but I started laughing at his comment. We sat and talked about fifteen minutes, and I suggested a cup of coffee. We drove around for a couple hours, not really looking for the cup of coffee. We did talk, and I no longer felt like a little girl. I was going to invite him home but figured it was better to save the invitation for another night. He touched me on the face and kissed me back before leaving the car. I remembered how soft his caress felt on my jaw all the way home.

He called me up the next day and asked me out on a "boy-girl" date. We dated for a couple months before I invited him home. I had been with several men through my fifty years of life, but none of them moved me the way that Jack did. He had an innate way of knowing just what to do. The more we dated, the more aggravating he got, and the more interesting he became.

After a year of dating, I started looking for more than what we had. Could this be my soul mate? I took a cruise with a girlfriend. It gave me a chance to think about Jack without his eyes distracting me. I found myself competing against Sarah, his wife. I realized he was still married to her in his mind, and I was a mistress. For an instant, I thought of ways I could steal him from her. How could I compete against someone who was dead? How could I be better than memories? These two questions summed up the dilemma. The more I thought about the situation between Jack and me, the more I wondered about Sarah. I had heard Jack talk about Sarah to others, but we only discussed her marginally.

I returned from vacation and told Jack what I was feeling. I explained that I felt like a mistress and I would never completely have him. Jack concurred with my assessment of our relationship. Part of me was hoping he would lie to me and tell me it was not true. Jack asked if we could still be friends. I had heard this line in the past and found previous lovers were only trying to stay near to me until I changed my mind. There was something very trusting in Jack, and I agreed to be friends.

I asked Jack to tell me about Sarah to satisfy my curiosity. His eyes sparkled as he talked about her. He liked to tell stories of the two of them together. I'd still meet with Jack once a week for business. Generally, the business would take fifteen minutes, and the rest of lunch, we talked about Sarah or our lives in general. His heart seemed lighter when he told his stories about her.

My favorite story was Sarah becoming CEO. Jack said, "Sarah and I were married a couple years, and I had worked for her father for ten years. Intricate Stamping Company was losing sales every year in a shrinking automotive market. I wanted to get into other markets, but her father refused. I was letting off steam to Sarah one night about the situation, and she said, 'Buy the business from Dad.' I thought she was either making a point or joking with me, but she was serious. Sarah was the only daughter of an only daughter and only had one daughter. When her grandfather passed away, he left his entire estate, a hundred thousand dollars, to Sarah. We were saving the money for retirement and promised each other not to spend it. Sarah insisted, and between the money I had saved and her inheritance, we had the down payment for the business. We went to her father, and he agreed to sell the business to us. I would've come to that conclusion on my own, but Sarah saw the writing on the wall and pushed me toward it. She stated since she put up most of the money to buy the company, she should be CEO, and I could have any other position I wanted. So remember, despite what you might hear from other people, I didn't make her CEO."

Jack should've been on Broadway with the stories he told about Sarah. You could see her strength and resolve as he illuminated her character. To hear Jack tell it, she was the boss of him. When you listened to his accounting of their lives, they shared equally in the marriage. I heard him say one time he was like a puppet on a string with her. I replied that his personality wouldn't let him be a puppet for anyone. I even reiterated some of his stories to show where they both got a lot and both gave a lot to the marriage. They had an understanding as to who was responsible in any given situation. I don't think it was anything spoken, yet power in the household was shared. I was married twice before and don't recall having our roles so well defined. Jack could only remember two serious arguments they ever had, and one was before they were married.

Sarah also had a playful side. Jack told me, "I was on the couch reading when Sarah laid on the couch next to me, with her feet on my lap. After a couple of minutes, she started rubbing my side and leg with her toes. It felt good but was somewhat annoying, since I was trying to read an article. This went on for about five minutes when she mischievously called out, 'Big dummy.' I turned and saw her blouse and pants undone. 'Big dummy' was her pet name for me when I missed the passes she threw at me. I asked where Katherine was. Sarah just said, 'Gone, left, out-of-here.' This news was a pleasant surprise for me."

Although Sarah was strong and playful, she was sentimental as well. My second favorite story Jack told was about being able to achieve the same results on their twentieth anniversary as they did on their wedding day. He put it into words this way: "The story begins in the spring of 1987. Sarah mentioned our twentieth anniversary was approaching and wanted to know what I had planned. 'It's only been twenty years?' I exclaimed. The comment almost slipped by without a response, but then she asked me if I'd like to rephrase my statement. I searched my mind for a quick save and came up with 'How about if we renew our vows?' I read in several articles of couples renewing their vows and saw a news blurb on the subject. The key to being a good husband is not how he can get into trouble; it is how much trouble he can get out of.

"We initially planned a small ceremony," he explained, "involving maybe ten people: family and close friends. Within a couple weeks, the number grew to over five hundred. Gail found out and invited herself. The next thing I knew, the whole office was attending. Terrell Jenkins mentioned it to the plant, and then the whole plant was coming. Sarah mentioned it at church, and many people wanted to attend. We decided to accommodate all who were interested. Sarah was a co-chairwoman for a house for unwed mothers. We asked that all gifts be directed to this charity. We ran into a snag when the pastor pointed out the church only held three hundred people. Being a mid-June event, the pastor suggested we have an outdoor wedding. We found a caterer who could manage this feat.

"The Monday before our vows," he continued, "Sarah took off my wedding band. It had been twenty years since

I took the ring off my finger, and it shrunk through the years. She explained that since she had no say-so in the wedding bands twenty years ago, she was buying the bands for this wedding. We were engaged on a Friday night, and the next morning, I went out and bought her a ring. It was my assumption the groom was supposed to buy the rings. I got a great deal by buying the engagement ring and both bands at the same time. Apparently, the bride is to pick the rings out; the groom just pays for them. Since I surprised her way back when, she was going to surprise me with these rings. I asked her about women hitting on me this week without my band. She told me to tell them I had a wife that could kick both our behinds.

"I was fine with wedding plans until the morning of the event," he said. "We had been married for twenty years, and yet there was anxiety surrounding the day. Katherine was Sarah's maid of honor. She chased me out of the house at nine o'clock, stating the groom shouldn't see the bride before the wedding. Ol' Joe, my best man, came by and picked me up. He and Sarah met in the spare room, where the wedding dress was laid out. He took me to his house, where we had a drink together. I asked to see Sarah's rings, and he indicated the damage that would befall him if he showed me. The rings would be a surprise.

"The wedding went smoothly, and we had a nice reception. Twenty years before, we got to our hotel room around one in the morning and lay on the bed, resting and talking. I remembered seeing the clock at 2 a.m. I dozed off for just a moment and woke up at five o'clock. The lights were all on, and Sarah was sleeping. I turned off the lights, and she woke me up at eight. She said I fell asleep;

she was going to turn off the lights, but she fell asleep too. The night of our second nuptials, we made it to the hotel at ten o'clock. We talked until she fell asleep at eleven."

"What about the rings?" I asked. "What was the surprise?"

"The pastor presided over the ceremony," he replied, "and when we got to the rings, she put mine on me first. It looked like the same ring, only new. It fit better, but I still hoped she didn't pay a lot for the rings. Then Ol' Joe handed me her rings. I opened the case and immediately recognized the rings. It was the engagement ring I bought twenty years earlier. One of the brackets that held the diamond in place broke off the first week she wore it. The same broken bracket was on the ring I placed on her finger. The pastor said she had something to say. I can still remember her words:

"'The jeweler where Jack bought the rings agreed to take them as trade-in on new rings. I went looking at the modest rings first. They were okay, but then I remembered how well we were doing and looked at the fine jewelry. I picked out a large diamond and two heavy bands. I was prepared to buy them. I made the mistake of opening the old boxes with our old rings. As the boxes opened, so did the memories with these rings. The jeweler must have seen the memories in my eyes because he offered to make the old rings look new. I told him not to fix the engagement ring; they led to twenty happy years, and they would lead us to another twenty years.'

"The pastor looked at me and asked if I had anything to say. I replied, 'No, she has said it all.' I asked her at bedtime why she didn't get the expensive jewelry and just keep the rings. She replied the other rings didn't have the luster our rings did. The next Christmas, I bought a very nice necklace for her from this jeweler."

Jack was also sentimental. He had a crusty outside he liked to show off. It didn't take much digging to see he was soft and tender under the thin membrane.

He told me, "When Katherine was twelve and entering the seventh grade, her interests changed. Sarah and Katherine were the best of friends and the worst of enemies. Half the time, they fought, and the other half, they told secrets. I wanted to stop Katherine from arguing with her mom, but Sarah said, 'No, stay out of it.' I told Sarah I felt left out of her life. We were finishing supper one night when Katherine mentioned math was giving her problems; she wanted her mother to help her. Sarah announced she was a poli-science graduate and knew nothing of math. If Katherine required help, she would have to see me. I thanked Sarah later for throwing me a bone. I knew she was very good in math and knew more about algebra than I ever did. I remembered taking it in junior high. I had to relearn the subject as I helped Katherine, but I spent time with her almost every night."

Jack and I were never intimate again, although the thought did cross my mind. We stopped seeing each other romantically in May 1998. We remained friends, and as a friend, I decided to surprise him on his birthday. I finished at the office at five o'clock and got to his house by six. Upon arriving, I noticed the house wide open. From the front door, I could see Jack, asleep on the couch. I noticed a bottle of whiskey less than half-full on the coffee table in front of him. There was an empty glass and an empty ice bucket to the other side of the bottle. At the other end of the coffee table was his wallet, keys, and reading glasses, stacked neatly in a pile.

Jack was lying twisted on the couch, as if he slumped over from a seated position. Wedged between him and the back of the sofa was a picture of Sarah. He had shown me this picture on several occasions; it was my impression it was his favorite.

He didn't need to go out, since it was quite apparent he had plenty to drink. I thought it best to get him into bed, where he would be more comfortable. I nudged him to wake up, which startled him. He snorted and then called out, "Sarah." Reality struck him, and he gave me a dazed look and said, "Oh, it's you."

I helped him upstairs to his room as he rambled on about not knowing I was coming.

I started to clean up the living room when I noticed some papers that were beneath him on the couch. In the papers, I found a newspaper clipping of Sarah's obituary. As I read the article, I realized they laid Sarah to rest on his birthday. I thought back and realized that I had never seen him on his birthday. I'd never seen him under the influence before that day, and I never saw him that way again. I also never tried to surprise him on his birthday again. He called me the next day to apologize for his drunken nature the night before.

Jack advised me on both personal and business matters. I learned a lot from him. He saw more potential in me than I saw in myself. I had been married twice and never held a job for more than two years. I had reached the point in my life where I thought I'd never hold a significant and meaningful position. I always blamed other people for my woes. All my life, I heard about a glass ceiling keeping women down and kept this concept as a security blanket. Whenever anything went wrong at a job, I could blame the glass ceiling. Without my consent, Jack showed me how to do better.

In my previous employments, I'd get home from work and think about everything I had done during the day and wonder if it was all worth it. Now, I get home from work and think about all the accomplishment during the day. The worth of my work is in the accomplishments. It doesn't matter how hard you work; the accomplishments are what's important. Jack taught me to be goal oriented as opposed to work oriented. Work without goals is meaningless.

I discovered changes in my personal relationships also. I met a man, and we started dating on a regular basis. My past relationships, if a problem or annoyance entered the relationship, I'd ignore it, in hopes of it going away. Jack showed me that by confronting these irritants as they happened, it keeps them from growing into cancers, eating away the relationship. All those debates with Jack taught me to remain calm and collected. One day, my sixteen-year-old niece told me I was a good listener. No one ever called me a good listener before. I married the man a month after Jack passed away. Through our positive conversations, we have defined our roles in the marriage.

Late in the morning of April 11, 2002, I was going through the first-quarter budget results that just arrived at my desk. Last January, Jack had predicted lower results from the year before because of 9/11. We had a 5 percent increase in revenue for the first quarter. It was first time Jack's predictions didn't come fruition. I thought to myself, *We will meet for lunch, and I can rub his nose in it.*

Jeannine, our new secretary, told me the chairman was on the phone. This immediately caused my heart to stop because he called so rarely. He told me he called so I didn't get the news elsewhere. My heart just sank in my chest, and it broke when he told me, "Jack passed away this morning." I'm sure he told me how, but it didn't register in my brain. I felt numb all over. I learned in a psych class that the human brain doesn't really go blank. It must think of something, but for a long moment, my mind was blank.

Jeannine, the new secretary, was in my office, calling for Kandi, when my brain activated again. I called everyone into the office for an impromptu meeting. I heard Jack talk about God in the past, and it never bothered me. He made it a point not to preach to me but always seemed to get a message to me about God. I was raised in a home where "God" was a word you used as an acceptable form of cussing. I don't know why, but I found myself asking this God of Jack's for help. A warm feeling came over me, and I told everyone about the phone call I just received.

I decided to close the office for the day; Jeannine offered to stay and answer the phone. I gave her a key to lock up at the end of the night. Jeannine had only met Jack on one occasion but understood the feeling the rest of us had for him. She said she would pray for us, and the warm feeling came over me again. The next couple of months, I went looking for that feeling again. I began by reading the Bible. I sought out the church Jack attended and met the preacher. He and I talked about God and Jesus all afternoon. When we were finishing, he asked if I wanted to pray the prayer of forgiveness and acceptance. I did the prayer with the preacher's help. I knew Jesus when I was finished.

My new husband, who asked me to keep him out the book, now attends church with me. I'm waiting patiently for God to touch him. I learned that by Jack passing away, there is good in dying. Only by dying can a person live with God. Jack's passing had one more benefit: me being saved. Jack was a good friend, lover, and business associate. I pray he and Sarah are together again.

Chapter 6
By Mary Osterhauf
(Jack's Last Girlfriend)

I was married for twenty years until 1990, when my husband left me for someone else. His leaving was all right by me. We hadn't lived as man and wife for some time. We even stopped fighting during the last years. After my youngest went to college, we divorced. The fact we got divorced hurt more than his leaving did. I moved to a small community south of Medina. The local church accepted me and helped me settle. I met briefly with Sarah Brown on several occasions. I met Jack once. I took a position with a hospice for terminally ill patients.

In 1997, the county hospital came to us and asked if we could help them set up a hospice for home care. Apparently, they received some equipment as a gift several years earlier. The hospital was not to charge for the use of the equipment. The hospital wanted to use this equipment for terminally ill patients wishing to die at home. They told us the equipment came from a donor named John Brown, who wife had died at home in 1991. It worked well for the family, and recently, another family made a similar request.

They assigned me to this family. Using the equipment, we set up a room at the home to care for the dying person. This person passed away just after the New Year started. Whole experience impressed both the family and the hospice administrators. We filed a report with hospital, and they were pleased with the outcome. They wanted to create an organization between them and us to help other families in this position. They asked me to head up this organization because I worked the home hospice and had the most knowledge on the subject.

The hospital set up a meeting between Mr. Brown and me. It turned out Mr. Brown was the same Jack Brown I met many years ago when I started at church. After socializing for a while, we got down to business. He pointed out all the benefits to a hospice at home. He also pointed out his advantage in life that allowed him to be with Sarah every day. When we finished the meeting, he told me to call anytime for help with this project.

Everyone agreed we would require some financial help if we were going to make this program available to average people and low-income families. When the insurance companies found out our project would cost less than a nursing home, they agreed to fund it. I heard Jack was influential in money-raising projects and asked him to help. He agreed to help set up a charitable company for this project. The two principle owners of the company would be the hospital and the hospice.

After a year of working on this project, Jack had a viable organization up and running. We had corporate donors and several fundraisers planned each year. I transferred to the company as technical advisor, and we got our first family to use our service. I made weekly trips to the house to refill the medicine dispenser, verify the patient's condition, and answer any questions. As the patient grew closer to the end, my visit became more frequent; I often stayed with the patient to relieve the family. At any given time, we had anywhere from two to five families participating in our home hospice.

Jack and I started dating in the summer of 1999. He asked me out after several hints by me and agreed to my terms. I insisted he return to church if we were going to date, even if he was a nonbeliever; I only dated men who attended church on a regular basis. I made an instant hit with his daughter by showing up one Sunday morning holding his arm. It was the first Sunday in September. I remember this because while everyone was taking communion, Jack was on his knees. The pastor dismissed the congregation, and everyone slowly meandered out of the worshipping hall, but Jack remained on his knees. I wanted to get going, and yet I knew not to disturb him. He knelt there as if he were in a trance. He was not praying or doing much of anything. Tears began to run down his face, and he continued to kneel. Fifteen minutes after service let out, he sat back in the chair next to me. He took a deep breath and cried, "That's what it's all about."

The pastor came over to see if he could help, and the three of us discussed the experience Jack just had. I've always believed in God; as far back as I can remember, God has been with me. I never knew how powerful the feeling of first meeting God could be. Jack always knew there was a God, and now he knew God loved him. Jack admonished the pastor for not telling him Jesus died on the cross for him personally. I thought it was insulting, but the pastor just chuckled as Jack smiled at him. I asked Jack about his comment later in the day, and he said there was not a Sunday where the pastor hadn't mentioned Jesus dying for him.

After this, Jack became more open about his emotions. On our dates, we talked about ourselves, including our exes. Our lives mirrored each other, except he had a magnificent marriage, and mine ended in tragedy. When he talked about Sarah, his heart seemed to float with joy. His blue eyes would twinkle with delight when animated with his speech.

I asked if there had ever been any troubled times between them. He explained the closest they came to having a tough time was the Friday after their first Thanksgiving.

He told the story this way: "I went to use the bathroom, and as usual, there was little to no paper on the roll. I thought it was a good thing to change the roll. About an hour later, Sarah came out of the bathroom, complaining how I put the roll on the spindle. She claimed the paper should come from behind, up and over, so you pull the paper from the top. When I was single, the paper was on either the sink counter or the back of the toilet. I only put it on the spindle when cleaning up for a date. To me, it was more important to have paper available to use than how it was on the roll.

"I should have left well enough alone and said okay, it won't happen again," he continued, "but I opened my mouth. 'I lived for four years in my own apartment,' I said, 'and in those four years, I used two rolls of paper, and the second was only half-used when I moved out. How did you manage to use a whole roll every week?' She spouted back that it lasted longer than a week. We bought a twelve-pack of paper on Labor Day, and Thanksgiving weekend, we needed more.

"'What, are you counting the sheets I use?' she demanded. 'No, but it's a lot to use' was my reply. 'I must dry myself every time I pee,' she explained. 'Do you have to wrap your hand like a mummy to do it?' I asked, which I clearly shouldn't have.

"Well, we got into it," he went on. "Every little annoyance we had for each other came out over the next couple of hours. I did this, and she did that. She wanted to know why I used so much soap while showering. At times, she was yelling at me, and at other times, we spoke quietly. During one of the extreme discussions, she said I must not love her if she was so terrible. This was the one and only time I ever raised my voice at her. I yelled back at her, 'Don't ever question my love again.' I didn't know why, but the comment really hurt. I walked outside and went into the garage. There was a bag of old clothes setting on the workbench, waiting to go to Goodwill. I punch it, slapped it, and started kicking it all around the garage.

"She came out about ten minutes later," he said, "and I was sitting on the hood of the car. She trembled with fear and approached me cautiously. I have this bar trick with my eyes when I get angry. It scares people and saved me from fights on several occasions. She apologized for her comment, and we hugged. I didn't know it at the time, but it was only the end of round one. We went inside and sat on the couch for an hour, not saying much of anything. Then I stuck my foot in it by saying, 'I don't know why it's so important to have the roll come from the top.' Round two had started. We argued most of the night and went to bed with a begrudging 'I love you' going both ways.

"Round three started on Saturday morning. It took me five months of living with her to learn how to lift the seat, and now she was complaining I didn't put the seat down. I told her she should put it up when she was done. She complained the porcelain was cold, and I asked if she dropped her britches while backing into the john. 'How else do you explain sitting on cold porcelain?' I asked. 'Even drunk, I've never sat on cold porcelain. Is that it? You've been drinking?' Well, we argued about the cold porcelain for a while, and then she brought up subjects that I thought were closed the day before.

"It was midafternoon," he continued, "and there was a calm in the storm. Her mother called, and Sarah answered the phone. She was pleasant and charming with her mother, after twenty-four hours of yelling at me. She told her mother everything was going great but she wouldn't be able to come for Sunday dinner.

"I did what I should have done from the very beginning and conceded the loss. I told her, 'There's nothing of any value we've been arguing about. I cannot promise to put the roll on the spindle properly. I cannot promise to put the seat down each time. I cannot promise to put my clothes in the hamper every time. What I can promise you is what I promised on our wedding day: I will love you until the day I die, plus eternity. I will try to remember all the things I cannot promise and try to accomplish these things, as you want.' I didn't know if I said something right or she was just tired of fighting, but she started crying and gave me a big hug. I did figure out why her comment on Friday hurt so much; it was because I loved her that much. I never took our love casually again. Thinking back, I believe this is what she was arguing. By me dismissing her wants, I was dismissing her.

"We made up that night and again on Sunday. On Monday morning, Mr. Sterling, my father-in-law, called me into his office. He said, 'I see the two of you made up.' I sat there for a moment, wondering how he knew. I guess he could tell by the look on my face and explained it was her mother's phone call on Saturday. Sarah was extraordinarily pleasant and civil with her mother. He pointed out the two were different because they were the same. They had bickered for the past ten years, and Sarah had never really been amiable to her mother in that time. He asked me if I gave into her and then answered, 'Of course you did; you made up.' He apologized to me for not remembering my dad passed away; he should have advised me on marriage. He told me when a man married a woman, he must remember one thing: 'Your behind belongs to her from that date forward.' There are certain things a wife is going to demand, and there are issues she's willing to negotiate, and there are a few items a man can determine. Your job as a husband is finding out what each is.'

"'Can't you just tell me?' I asked. Dad replied, 'That's the fun of being married: finding out who is in charge.' He added Sarah and her mother were probably talking right now about us. They will be friends now Sarah has a common problem with her mother: hardheaded husbands. I mentioned the toilet paper; he laughed and said, 'Come from behind, up and over so you pull the paper from the top.' Dad added if I wanted to know what Sarah would be like in twenty-five years, look at her mother. Whenever Sarah and I were picking on each other, I always had the trump of calling her Elena, her mother's name."

This was the first time I heard him admit how much he loved her. You could tell how much he loved her by the stories he told, but now he was admitting it. When he finished telling the story, there was a pregnant pause and he gasped, "I still love her and miss her." I work with families who have a person dying, and Jack seemed to be going through the stages of grief. He was starting to let her go after more than eight years.

One time, I saw the bar trick he did with his eyes. There was an elderly couple using our service. She had been fighting cancer for five years, and recently, the doctors admitted there was nothing more they could do for her. She told her doctor she wanted to finish her life at home, if possible. The doctor referred her to us. We met with her and her husband. He would retire to be with her at the end. Their daughter lived in Medina, which was about fifteen miles from their house. Their son was still in the navy, stationed in San Diego.

Once a week, I'd relieve the man, and a friend of his would pick him up, and they'd leave the house. His daughter periodically came over and relieved him. This was working without problems until the son returned from California for a visit. His mother just started IV treatment for the pain. We got a call one Friday, asking for our help. Jack picked me up and drove me over there.

The son came out to meet us by cussing at us. He told me we were not wanted and we should just go back to where we came from. I looked at the father, who was almost in tears. Jack stayed in the car, as I instructed him to do. I was trying to talk with the young man about his mother's condition, but he was getting more and more belligerent. He kept calling his dad a cheapskate who wouldn't spend the money to save his mom.

I tried to say something, and he got in my face and proceeded to curse at me. The next thing I knew, Jack jumped in between us. He stated coldly, "Back off," and the big guy backed off. We had a fundraiser a couple of months before, and several members of the Cleveland Browns were there. This was how big the son was, and Jack got him to back up. Jack continued to speak at him in a voice that was totally devoid of any emotion. The look on the son's face blazed with the fear of death. Whatever Jack did with his eyes scared the big man. His father, who had feared for our safety, now feared for his son's. He pled with Jack not to harm him.

Jack's voice gained compassion as the son started to listen to reason. The police showed up but stayed back and watched the events unfold. The officer seemed captive to Jack's words.

He told the son, "Your mom is mostly dead. Cancer has eaten a good portion of her body. Your mom chose to live out her final days in the house she called home for over forty years. All you have left is your dad. Have you thought of what your dad is going through? I know what he's going through because I lost my Sarah the same way, almost ten years ago. Picture you're losing your wife; go on, close your eyes, and picture her with cancer, and the doctors all say there is nothing more they can do. That is your mother dying in the house. She stopped being number one to you when you married your wife. She's still number one to your father. I see an old woman dying in the house, but your father sees the love of his life dying in the house. Instead of supporting your father, you want to rip his heart out by not allowing him to grant your mother's last wish: to die in the house she calls home. You're tearing her away from the memories of raising you into a strong man, your sister to a wonderful mom, and growing old with your father. Now you want to take that from her and your father. You said you had the money to save her. Go, offer it to your mother, and see what she tells you. Go, give her the money, and write the check. I promise you this: Your father would give everything he owned to save your mother. He would be willing to live in a cardboard box if it would save your mother."

When Jack finished his sermon, the son was in tears. His father stood with his arms opened wide, and the son fell into the father's chest, weeping uncontrollably. I turned to the officer, and he had his hankie out, brushing his nose. I asked if there was to be any action taken. The officer cleared his throat and choked, "It depends on us." The officer said there was no evidence of any violence. If no one wanted to press charges, his work was done. The old man took a hand off his son's back and waved the cop away. We went in to check on the mother, and she had slept through the whole incident. The father demanded, "No one tells Mother about what happened here today."

Later, the father thanked Jack for his help. The two talked quietly for a while. When the son finished visiting with his mother, he hugged Jack and apologized to everyone for his behavior. I talked with the daughter a couple of days later. She asked if Jack made the story up, or did he really live it? I assured her it was all too real for him.

A couple weeks after Jack's salvation, we went to eat at a restaurant he half-owned. A year before, a young man approached Jack with an idea for a restaurant. This young man told me a couple weeks after Jack passed away about how he got in business with Jack. The young man trained in New York to be a chef. He worked a restaurant there for several years and saved up some money. He was never happy in New York and decided to move back to Medina. He had an idea to open a New York-style restaurant in Medina but needed more capital to do so. He presented several predominant businessmen a written business plan to achieve his goals. Jack was the only one who called him. Jack verbally ripped his plans to shreds. After that, the cost for opening his dream went from two hundred thousand dollars to three hundred thousand dollars. The young man financed 50 percent through a bank, and Jack became 50 percent owner of the restaurant. There was a survivor benefit written into the agreement. The young man is now donating Jack's profits to several charities in the community.

After dinner, Jack ordered his usual drink, a glass of twelve-year-old Jack Daniels with two ice cubes in it. I never saw him empty the glass, but he liked to sip it over time. I was curious and asked how it was. He slid the glass over and told me to try it. My face must have shown my disdain, and he told me to swirl my finger in the glass and taste my finger. At his insistence, I swirled and tasted. It was surprisingly good.

I could tell there was something eating at him and asked why he agonized over Sarah after all these years. He explained that on more than one occasion, he had asked God, why her? He was the one who drank and cussed; why her? Jack often wondered if he believed in God, would she still have to die so young? She had deep faith in God; he could see it in her eyes.

He said, "Since I met her, I've wanted the feeling she had when praying to God. If she had the faith, I figured we would both be okay. I tried to fill the emptiness of not knowing God with her love. Lucky for me, the love I had for her was strong enough to fill most of the void. I don't pretend to know the mind of God, but I speculated he might have taken her to show me even her love can leave me, and only his love is eternal. For as long as she was alive, my heart was not open to anything else. Sometimes, I feel it was my lack of faith that killed her. After she died, I knew if we were going to be together again, I'd have to find God. I would pray to him to let me be with Sarah throughout eternity. I'd try to make deals with God. I was willing to give all I owned, all I ever would make, to charity, if he would just let me be with her. All that did was to show me God couldn't be bought.

"Someone told me to talk with God," he continued, "and I tried it. I begged and pleaded with God to be with Sarah again. I reasoned, 'I even do your work, and yet nothing.' You talked me into attended church again, and that only showed me how grave the situation had become.

I wanted God to choose me. I was a willing volunteer for him. A few weeks ago, while sitting in church, I asked God, 'Why not me? I'm a proud man who will serve you proudly.' I got to my wits' end and finally had nothing more to add. I told myself, if I get no reply, I will resolve not to be with God. I sat there in my chair, waiting for a response.

"Then thoughts of why would God want my money crossed my mind. God is God and doesn't need anything I can give him. This thought really hurt me. Nothing I can do or say will impress God. Then I thought, *How do I get to heaven?* I looked up, and the pastor was pointing at the cross. He said, 'Get down on your knees and pray.' I got on my knees and stared at the cross. I started thinking of the sacrifice Jesus made for everyone. Then I heard Sarah's voice say, 'For you, big dummy.' I was a big dummy. I realized God didn't want anything but my heart, my love, and me, unconditionally. No deals and no bargains. I'd have to love him, his way.

"In a way," he went on, "Sarah saved me again. She always knew when I was hurting. If something was bothering me, I could hide it from everyone but her. She had a habit of making me discuss whatever was bothering me. It was as if I was transparent, and she could see exactly what it was and made me talk about it. When we first bought Intricate Stamping Company, we had some tough times. Money was tight, and getting into new markets wasn't as easy as I thought. I worried about losing the company. She held me tight one night and told me not to worry; it was in God's hands. I cried like a baby in her arms. Whether I was sick, worried, or scared, she was there for me. That day, she was there for me again. I realized her voice was me remembering, but she was there for me. She shut me up and made me listen to God. By God's grace and the love of Jesus for me, I am saved."

Jack drank the rest of the libation and slammed his glass on the table. Tears started running down his face. He sat, stoned-faced and silent. I think he was waiting for me to say something, but I was drawing a blank. I pulled all the cash I had out of my purse, threw it on the table, and suggested we go for a walk (I found out the next day Jack had a tab, and the owner returned the money to me). We walked for a while before Jack said anything. Then he said it was a nice night for a walk. I thought it was a little cold but agreed with what he said.

I concluded that night I'd have to share Jack with Sarah. To separate Sarah and Jack was impossible. Jack was who he was because of Sarah. To ask him to give up Sarah would be asking him to give up part of who he was. He would never be over her, and I didn't want to become her, either. For me to try to fill Sarah's position in his life, I'd have to destroy who I was. I think Jack kept the other women in his life at arm's distance to protect his memories of Sarah. I noticed the next day that Jack had taken off his ring. I believe he realized no matter what happened in his life, he would always have those twenty-five years he spent with Sarah.

When Sarah died, it left a huge void in his life. When he found Jesus and accepted him as his savior, this filled the void and put his heart to rest. He no longer needed to cling to the memory of Sarah for his happiness. Only God could make him give up his illusory love for Sarah. We got much closer in the next couple of years. On September 12,

2001, the whole country was in shock from the day before. Jack brought me lunch, and we talked through the meal.

He told me there was something he wanted to say: "When Sarah died, I couldn't see me loving another person. I had two deep loves in my life: Sarah and Katherine. With Sarah gone, it left me with one love: Katherine. The Thanksgiving after Sarah died, Katherine was getting ready to go to college, and it dawned on me: I wouldn't be seeing her as much. I made it a point to start telling her how much I loved her. We used to have this game of saying 'Luv ya' to each other. Starting that morning, I started saying, 'I love you,' to her, so she would know how much I loved her. With the attack on the country and the uncertainty of war approaching us, I think it's important to tell you, I love you. You've meant a lot to me over the last couple of years. I didn't want the chance for me to tell you to slip away. I love you."

For the first time in my life, I was speechless. Before I knew what happened, the subject changed, and we were talking about the impending war. Before he left, I did tell him, "I love you too." For a moment, I thought he was going to ask me to marry him. The subject never came up again.

April 10, 2002, was a busy day for me. Along with my scheduled stops for the day, a family living at the edge of the county asked if I could make a special trip to see them. I had to go by the office to get home, and it was right at five o'clock, so I decided to stop. The secretary ran out to the car and said she had a message for me. She had been trying to get me on my cell phone. I always turn it off when I'm with a family and sometimes forget to turn it back on afterward. She told me Katherine called and said Jack was sick in the hospital, and she needed me. I was expecting a severe flu, injury, or some ailment. Sarah and Brian were at the cardiac ICU when I arrived. Sarah asked me to meet with the doctor and explain to her what was happening with her father.

The doctor was the top cardiologist in the county. I had worked with him in the past in conjunction with the hospice. The doctor pointed out Jack wouldn't require my service. He explained to me in medical details exactly what was wrong with Jack. It was worse than Katherine had mentioned to me. The doctor, confused by the problem, wondered why there was no detection of the condition. The defect in his heart was obvious and easily repairable. Jack was a master of hiding his problems. I had dated him for two years and hadn't noticed any signs of him having difficulty. Both the doctor and I were surprised that Jack lasted until the next morning.

Brian handled all the arrangements for Jack's burial. He called me the day after Jack passed away and asked me about Jack's girlfriends. He mentioned several of them had called and seemed quite upset at his passing. Brian wanted to know if I was aware of these women and if I could point them out. Jack had discussed all his past girlfriends, including the indiscretions he had with them. I explained there were only three women who been intimate with Jack and remained good friends with him. I gave Brian the name of these women and their phone numbers. Brian wanted to invite anyone who knew Jack closely to a private viewing.

Jack mentioned the three other women who occupied

his time before me. He went into detail of what they meant to him and the blessing they had been in his life. He deeply regretted having sex with these women, especially after finding Christ. He said their relationship would have been just as deep without sleeping with them. His crass human behavior caused him to sleep with them. It was one of the many weaknesses of being a man. He prayed with me one time that his sexual weakness would have no ill effects for them. He knew it left some difficulties in their lives. They all had the dilemma of sleeping with Jack and then having a new boyfriend. What do you tell them? How do you explain your past indiscretions? With Bonnie and Marybeth, how could they explain their sins to their children?

I met the three women on separate occasions in the past. I admit it was nice when Jack introduced me as his girlfriend. I ran into all of them again at the different venues in Jack's honor. I asked if we could share the grieving process by meeting somewhere. To my astonishment, they all agreed. I was talking with Katherine at the burial site, and she mentioned her disappointment in not knowing the women who were in her dad's life. I told her about the social planned that night. She seemed uncertain about coming, and Brian suggested she go. Two years after Jack's death, we are all still friends.

One of the questions that plagued me was, "Who was Jack's doctor?" I asked Katherine about it, and she said her family doctor was the son of her doctor when she was growing up. I met with this doctor, and he explained he had never seen Jack. I received a call from the doctor about two weeks later, and he said they found Jack's file

DANIEL MACPHERSON

in the basement. The last recorded visit for Jack was 1957, when he came in with a broken nose. I checked the county hospital, and they had no record of Jack visiting the hospital. I called every doctor in and about our small town, but no one had a record of Jack visiting. This explained why there was not an early detection of his condition.

Jack was very special to me. When around him, it was hard not to focus on him because he made you feel like you were the only person in the room. I had given up on having a meaningful relationship before he came into my life. After my divorce, I had buried myself in work and church to avoid the disappointment of not having a man in my life. Jack showed me I could love again and got me to forgive myself for my divorce and the terrible marriage I had. I will miss you, Jack.

Age of People for Specific Events					
Date	Jack	Sarah	Katherine	Mr. Sterling	Ol' Joe
Born	9/10/1943	7/2/1944	8/16/1973	4/28/1913	2/1/1924
06/01/41				28	17
08/08/61	17	17	N/B	48	37
06/16/67	24	24	N/B	54	43
09/14/72	29	28	N/B	59	48
08/16/73	29	29	0	60	49
11/08/81	38	37	8	68	57
06/13/87	43	42	13	74	63
09/05/91	47	47	18	78	67
09/06/92	48		19	79	68
09/12/93	50		20	80	69
06/22/97	53		23	84	73
09/14/98	55		25	86	75
09/05/99	55		26	86	75
04/11/02	58		28	88	78

Date	Event	Date	Event
06/01/41	Ol' Joe Goes into Army	09/05/91	Sarah Dies
08/08/61	Jack Starts at ISC	09/06/92	Jack Meets Bonnie
06/16/67	Jack and Sarah Marry	09/12/93	Jack Meets Marybeth
09/14/72	They Buy ISC	06/22/97	Jack Dates Eddie
08/16/73	Katherine Is Born	09/14/98	Jack Meets Mary
11/08/81	Jack Gets Sick	09/05/99	Jack Finds God
06/13/87	Jack and Sarah Renew Vows	04/11/02	Jack Dies

Printed in the United States
By Bookmasters